Rilla murmured something, and rocked her head from side to side, but didn't waken.

Luca sighed and hunkered down beside her. He lifted a hand to shake her shoulder, but was caught by the protective way her fingers were splayed down low on her belly.

His baby lay beneath that hand. Their baby. He shook his head at the wonder of it all and gave in to the urge to lie down beside her. He lay on his side, his elbow bent, his head propped on his hand, and gazed down at her.

He would never have thought he'd get a second chance at this. Never. When things had ended between them he hadn't even been able to contemplate something this wonderful ever happening again. The end had been too painful, too soul-destroying for him to ever want to be here again. But he was. And he wanted to hold his baby so badly he couldn't resist putting his hand out to touch her.

Dear Reader

Welcome to Brisbane General Hospital! Set in my home town of Brisbane, this trilogy explores the lives and loves of three nurses, the Winters sisters—Beth, Rilla and Hailey. And three very special doctors—Gabe, Luca and Callum.

I've always wanted to write a linked series, and was thrilled when my editor suggested it. I love catching up with previous characters and being familiar with a particular setting. And Brisbane General is a beauty. Being a nurse, I can tell you there's no place quite like a hospital to bring out real emotions and make people realise what is truly important in life.

In DR ROMANO'S CHRISTMAS BABY, it's Rilla and Luca's turn. Rilla's carefully ordered world is turned upside down when, after seven years apart, her gorgeous husband Luca reappears as Brisbane General's new Director of Emergency Medicine. The seething sexual tension between them cannot be denied—and neither is prepared for the consequences. Will Rilla and Luca get a much deserved happily-ever-after in their Christmas stockings? I hope you enjoy finding out.

Don't miss Hailey's story coming in July from Mills & Boon® Medical™.

Amy Andrews

DR ROMANO'S CHRISTMAS BABY

BY
AMY ANDREWS

MILLS & BOON®
Pure reading pleasure™

First published in Great Britain 2008
Large Print edition 2009
Harlequin Mills & Boon Limited,
Eton House, 18-24 Paradise Road,
Richmond, Surrey TW9 1SR

© Amy Andrews 2008

ISBN: 978 0 263 20511 4

Set in Times Roman 16¾ on 19¾ pt.
17-0509-48840

Printed and bound in Great Britain
by CPI Antony Rowe, Chippenham, Wiltshire

Amy Andrews has always loved writing, and still can't quite believe that she gets to do it for a living. Creating wonderful heroines and gorgeous heroes and telling their stories is an amazing way to pass the day. Sometimes they don't always act as she'd like them to—but then neither do her kids, so she's kind of used to it. Amy lives in the very beautiful Samford Valley, with her husband and aforementioned children, along with six brown chooks and two black dogs. She loves to hear from her readers. Drop her a line at www.amyandrews.com.au

Recent titles by the same author:

TOP-NOTCH SURGEON, PREGNANT NURSE*
THE OUTBACK DOCTOR'S SURPRISE BRIDE
FOUND: A FATHER FOR HER CHILD
THE ITALIAN COUNT'S BABY

Brisbane General Hospital

To my sister-in-law Emily,
one of my biggest supporters.
And to all those health care professionals
who man our hospitals over Christmas while
everyone else is making merry.
Extra-special Christmas joy to all of you.

CHAPTER ONE

'I CAN'T believe I've still got a month to go,' Beth puffed disgustedly as her legs plodded on down the bushy track, her hand kneading the small of her back. 'I feel like I've been pregnant for ever. Now I know how elephants feel.'

Rilla looked at her sister and stifled a laugh. She'd never seen Beth look more beautiful. 'Pregnancy becomes you,' she said, patting her sister's swollen belly.

Rilla felt a rush of emotion at the firm swelling beneath her hand and a twinge in her chest that had nothing to do with the exertion of the walk.

Beth shot Rilla a don't-patronise-the-expectant-mother look. 'Oh, yeah. Morning sickness, heartburn, backache and varicose veins. Very becoming,' Beth muttered. 'And to top it off I've got this damn head cold.' She blew her nose on a tissue. 'I mean, who gets a cold in September, for crying out loud?'

Rilla laughed, startling a nearby parrot, which took to the air with an indignant cry and a blur of crimson wings. 'You should be at home with your feet up, not trampling through the bush with me.'

'I'm going stir-crazy at home with nothing to do. I could have still been at work but Gabe insisted I take the full six weeks' maternity leave.'

'He likes to fuss.' Rilla shrugged.

'He's driving me mad.'

Rilla grinned at the thought of her brother-in-law in full don't-even-lift-a-paperclip mode. She stumbled over a tree root hidden beneath a carpet of leaf litter and fell behind Beth a little. She looked up to see her sister steaming ahead, still tall and straight as a stick from behind, despite the advanced pregnancy.

So unlike her own shorter, curvier proportions. Rilla had no doubt she'd be well up to the waddling stage by now. *If only.*

'Anyway, I'm sick of talking about me. Let's talk about something else.'

'OK, sure.' Rilla shrugged again. 'What do you want to talk about?'

'Let's talk about you.'

Rilla frowned. 'What about me?'

'We're worried about you, Ril.'

Rilla looked at her older sister. 'We?'

'The family. All of us.'

Rilla groaned. She'd been set up. 'So you're the emissary, are you?'

'Come on, Ril. We love you. Of course we worry. You've been working hard for years to get the NUM job but the last few months, since the position came up, you've been working yourself into the ground. Then there was all the stress of the interview last week. Not to mention the divorce papers and taking off your wedding ring. We all know what a big step that was for you. If you're not careful, you'll be heading for a breakdown.'

'I'm fine,' Rilla said testily.

'You don't sound like it. Maybe you need to talk about it? About him?' Beth said gently.

'I do not want to talk about Luca,' Rilla said tersely.

She didn't even want to think about her estranged husband. The fact that she would be working with him again in a couple of weeks was causing enough angst. Only a matter of days until her world would once again tilt on its axis.

'Have you heard from him yet? Where's he going to be living?' Beth persisted.

'I suppose back at the flat…I don't know. And I don't care. I have better things to do than think about Luca Romano,' Rilla retorted.

'Which is why we're walking to the very waterfall where he proposed to you eight years ago,' Beth pointed out.

'Hey,' Rilla protested. 'You wanted to go for a bush walk. I'm not David Attenborough. This is the only one I know.'

Beth raised an eyebrow. 'It just seems a little… Freudian,' she suggested.

The irony of their destination hadn't been lost on her either, but Rilla refused to dignify her sister's statement with a comment. The memories of the day Luca had brought her here were particularly powerful as she walked along.

So much so she could swear she caught the occasional whiff of the unique aftershave Luca had always favoured.

They walked in silence for a few moments. The smell of eucalyptus, wattle and damp earth mingled to form a unique bushy fragrance. The heavy warmth of the September day was tempered by the thick canopy above. It filtered the sun's intensity, allowing only a sprinkle of sunlight to bathe the path.

A bellbird tinkled in the background, complementing the persistent hum of insect song. A kookaburra laughed in the distance. The track was deserted on this Friday morning but come tomorrow it would be bustling with weekend tourists and city slickers keen for a slice of the great outdoors.

'So he starts in a fortnight?' Beth asked.

Rilla sighed and resigned herself to a grilling. 'Apparently.'

'And you haven't heard a word from him?'

'I haven't spoken to Luca in seven years, you know that.'

Not since he'd gone back to Italy after they'd

both acknowledged it was over. Even the divorce papers had been handled via his lawyer. 'If Dad hadn't told me, I wouldn't even have known he'd applied for the job.'

Beth whistled. 'Seven years. That's a long time.'

'Tell me about it,' Rilla griped, feeling every day of the intervening years.

Beth put her arm around Rilla. 'It's such a big step—divorce. I know it hasn't been easy for you, Ril. Are you OK?'

Rilla felt tears prick at her eyes. 'Sure,' she said huskily.

They walked in silence for a few minutes. Beth stopped to hold her stomach as she sneezed and Rilla waited for her to blow her nose and resume their pace.

'Why now? For the papers?' Beth asked, under way again. 'You never really said.'

Rilla shrugged. 'I guess it's like you and Hails have been saying—I need closure. I think turning thirty a few months ago made me realise that I'm not young any more. I want to get married and have a baby. Seeing you pregnant had really bought that home.'

Rilla's arm brushed against her sister's pregnant girth and she felt a deep well of longing rise within her and tears threatened again. The miscarriage she'd had at twenty-two hurt more acutely than ever. The thought of never fulfilling her biological purpose was deeply, deeply devastating.

'I'm just in this kind of…limbo. I think I've finally recognised that I need to draw that part of my life to a close and get on with the rest of it. I can't go forward with my past dragging me back all the time.'

Rilla felt Beth's arm tighten around her shoulders and she felt immensely comforted as they trudged along the track.

'And so pretty soon you're going to be seeing him every day,' Beth stated a few minutes later.

'Yes,' Rilla agreed, feeling utterly miserable. The sadness and guilt and tumult as their fledgling marriage had fallen apart seemed suddenly magnified by their absolute silence over the intervening years.

She'd thought she was over their brief, albeit intense relationship. Thought she was past it.

She'd finally filed for divorce, hadn't she? But his imminent reappearance was unsettling.

'Maybe there's a chance you two will…'

Rilla stopped walking and turned to Beth. She felt the years slip away. All the hurt and pain coming back in one violent rush.

'Too many years have gone by, Beth. We were like strangers at the end. We shouldn't have rushed in like we did, and getting pregnant so soon…'

She looked at Beth's belly, swollen with Gabe's baby and felt a stab of jealousy mix with her despair over the loss of Luca's baby. She wasn't twenty-two any more and Rilla wished for the hundredth time she could go back and live that time over again.

'We were doomed from the beginning.'

'He hasn't signed the papers, though, has he?' Beth countered.

Rilla shrugged, at a loss to explain why he hadn't. She'd been expecting him to initiate proceedings years before and she'd most certainly expected him to sign the papers and end their dead-as-a-doornail marriage posthaste.

'Maybe he regrets the things that happened?

That he withdrew from you? He was hurting, Rilla,' Beth said gently.

Rilla knew how much her family had adored her husband despite their initial qualms over the hasty match. And Beth in particular had always had a soft spot for Luca.

'So was I.'

Beth put her arm around Rilla's shoulders again. 'I know. Come on.' She pulled Rilla along with her. 'We're nearly there. I can hear the water.'

They came into a shady clearing carved from the thick bush land dominated by water cascading down a massive rock face into a crystal-clear pool beneath. Big flat boulders edged the waterhole. A slight breeze ruffled the tops of the canopy and revealed glimpses of an azure sky and cotton-wool clouds.

'Wow, this is beautiful!' Beth exclaimed in a hushed awe.

It was lush and vibrant. The abundant foliage looked as if it had been there since the dawn of time, its dark green opulence like a magical jewel, whispering of ancient times. Birdsong echoed around the still clearing, which was like a prehistoric amphitheatre, rustling through the leaves with a resonance more magnificent than a choir of angels.

It was perfect. A testament to the creativity of Mother Nature. Rilla felt as if they'd walked into the Garden of Eden. It was hard to imagine that such a paradise could exist in the centre of a thriving city, Mt Cootha being a mere ten-minute drive from the CBD.

'I'd forgotten how beautiful it is here,' Rilla said, her quiet voice invading the vibrant stillness.

'Well, Luca always did have an eye for beautiful things,' Beth said, grinning at her sister.

Rilla smiled a watery smile and they stood arm in arm, absorbing the wild beauty for a few moments.

'Come on.' Rilla roused herself. 'Let's sit.'

Beth nodded. 'I brought some sandwiches and cool drinks.'

They took their shoes and socks off and Rilla supported Beth as she lowered herself down to one of the many smooth boulders that formed a natural rim to the pool.

'Oh, God, I'm never going to get up again,'

Beth sighed as she dipped her legs into the blissfully cool water. She reached into her pocket for her tissue and blew her nose again. 'I must look like a beached whale.'

Rilla smiled. Beth was full and ripe and lush. She placed her hand over the sudden ache that had sprung from her womb. 'Don't moan, whale,' Rilla teased, to disguise the bleakness inside. 'I'll help you.'

'You'll need a crane,' Beth said.

'Stop fishing for compliments,' Rilla said bossily, plonking herself down next to Beth. 'You're blooming.'

'Tell that to my back,' Beth grumbled as she accepted a bottle of water from her sister.

'It seems to be bothering you a bit.'

'It's been bothering me for months,' Beth said dismissively as she took a long pull of cool water. 'It doesn't help that this rock is so damn hard it could put diamond to shame.'

'You're right.' Rilla laughed, preparing to get up. 'We don't have to stay. We can head back.'

Beth put a stilling hand on her sister's arm. 'Are you kidding? It's like paradise here. I want to just sit and absorb it for a while. And I need a rest.'

Rilla relented. The trek hadn't been particularly arduous, a little uneven and rocky in places, but, then, she wasn't walking for two.

'I know you don't want to talk about Luca, Ril. But being proposed to here must have been very, very romantic.'

Rilla trailed her legs through the water as she thought back to that magical day. Had it only been eight years ago? It seemed like decades. But then some days, like today, it came back to her in such vivid detail it could have been yesterday.

'Yes, it was.'

They had been alone here that day too. She remembered the feeling of isolation, of feeling they were the only two people in the world wrapped up in a cocoon of love. And she remembered the feeling of absolute rightness. That even after only three months she and Luca were meant to be. That nothing could put them asunder.

It had been a day full of promise and hope.

The future had been so bright. So positive. She'd had no inkling that only seven months later their dreams would be crushed into the dirt and within a year it would all be over.

'Got any Vegemite and cheese?' Rilla asked, rousing herself from the memories that seemed to have taken over her life since finding out about Luca's return.

'Of course,' Beth said, passing a round of Rilla's favourite sandwiches to her.

They sat with their legs dangling in the pool, munching on sandwiches, chatting and laughing as the water trickled down the rock, inexorably eroding the surface. They didn't talk about Luca, or the baby. In fact, sometimes they didn't even talk at all, familiar enough with each other to be comfortable with silence. They mightn't share the same DNA but they were as close as any blood sisters.

'Damn,' Beth muttered, rubbing her back again. 'I think I'm going to have to get up. My back's on fire and my butt is numb.'

They packed up their wrappers and Rilla helped Beth get her shoes back on.

'God, I can't wait to see my feet again.' Beth grimaced as Rilla hauled her upright. 'Ow,' she called, reaching out to her sister as she doubled over.

'What?' Rilla demanded.

'Oh, no.' Beth's grip tightened as she looked down.

Rilla looked down also. To her dismay a rapidly spreading wet patch stained the front of Beth's shorts.

'I think my membranes just ruptured,' Beth said.

Rilla exchanged a look with her sister.

'Oh, boy. Gabe's not going to be happy,' Beth said.

Rilla couldn't have agreed more as she stared at the fluid now leaking down Beth's leg.

'It can't be happening now. I've still got four weeks to go. It's too soon. What are we going to do?'

'It's OK,' Rilla said, hearing the first note of panic in her older sister's voice. She was a nurse. She'd delivered the odd baby or two, the ones that couldn't wait. *Not that it was going to come to that.*

'It's fine. We have plenty of time. Are you having contractions?'

Beth shook her head. 'No. Just Braxton-Hicks' on and off the last few days. It's mainly my back.'

Rilla gaped at her sister and bit back an exasperated retort. It seemed very likely that Beth had been dismissing true contractions for the harmless Braxton-Hicks' variety. She didn't want to think about the fact that they'd been blissfully walking through the bush while Beth was in labour.

'I wish Hailey was here too,' Beth murmured.

Ditto. Beth would have been far better off having their youngest sister here. Rilla certainly would have given anything to have someone who had delivered hundreds of babies by their side. But Hailey had declined to join them today, out searching for apartments to rent instead.

'OK, here's what we're going to do,' Rilla announced. 'We're going to get back to the car as quickly as possible and then we're going to drive straight to the General. It won't even be a ten-minute drive from here. OK?'

'OK.' Beth nodded.

Rilla took an arm and let Beth lean against her as they left the waterhole. They hadn't gone ten paces when Beth stopped abruptly, practically crippled by a contraction.

'I don't think that was Braxton-Hicks',' Beth said, her voice wobbling.

Rilla felt Beth's arms trembling and did some calculations in her head. The walk to the waterhole had taken thirty minutes. The return trip would take longer if they had to keep stopping for contractions. Her heart slammed madly like an open shutter in the middle of a force ten gale.

'Tell me it's going to be OK, Rilla,' Beth gasped, her hold on Rilla tightening.

Rilla could hear the tremble in her sister's voice. Beth who was always cool, calm and collected was looking to her for assurance. Beth, who, prior to her maternity leave, had run the operating theatres at the General like a sergeant major for years.

'Of course it is,' she said confidently. 'First baby labours take for ever.' That was one piece of information she did remember in a brain that seemed to be suddenly frozen.

'But it's not my first baby.' Beth grimaced as she clutched at her stomach.

Of course—it wasn't. 'It may as well be,' Rilla said reassuringly. 'Twenty-three years is a long time. We wipe the slate clean after a while. How long was your labour with David?'

'Four hours,' Beth said through gritted teeth.

Rilla tried not to look too alarmed when she glanced sharply at her older sister. 'Let's hustle,' she said, kicking up the pace.

But the going was still slow. The contractions increased in frequency and length over the next twenty minutes, necessitating the need for numerous stops and Rilla was becoming more worried that they weren't going to make it to the General.

The track remained deserted and their mobile phones still had no signal. All they could do was trudge on and hope the premature baby didn't decide to make an appearance.

Rilla judged they were about twenty minutes from the car when Beth let out a cry and gripped hard to the arm that was supporting her.

'What?' Rilla demanded.

'Oh, God,' Beth panted. 'I need to push.'

'No. No, no, no,' Rilla said, shaking her head wildly. 'No pushing. It's not far now.'

'Ril,' Beth said, leaning forward. 'I think the baby's right there.'

'No.'

'Yes,' Beth said looking her younger sister straight in the eye. 'It is. This baby is coming. Now.'

Rilla believed her. *Oh, no!* It was time to go to plan B. 'OK.' *Don't panic. Just do what has to be done.* 'I'll get the picnic blanket out of the backpack. I think we need to take a look.'

Rilla's pulse thundered as she spread the blanket on the track and helped Beth to the ground. This was Beth. Her sister. And her niece. The stakes couldn't be higher and she was scared out of her brain.

'Hurry,' Beth bellowed loudly.

The loud groan broke into Rilla's escalating fear. 'OK, Beth, let's take a look,' Rilla said, forced to focus as the sound of her sister's agony echoed through the bush.

* * *

Luca Romano was taking a walk down memory lane when he heard the cry of distress nearby. He responded immediately, pistoning his strong legs and arms hard to reach the source. Someone was obviously in trouble. The cry had been full of pain and panic. The bush grew eerily quiet as he headed towards the sound, as if it too could detect the urgency of the situation.

He burst from a side track onto the main pathway, locating the problem with a quick swivel of his neck to the right. He cursed under his breath. Two women were huddled on the track. *What the hell had happened?*

'Everything all right here?' he asked as he approached.

Rilla's head snapped up. She may have had her back to the approaching man but she'd have known that sexily accented voice anywhere. It still haunted her dreams and stoked her fantasies. She turned. *Of all the men in the entire world, their knight in shining armour had to be him?*

'Luca?'

Beth also looked up. 'Luca?'

Luca stopped dead in his tracks. 'Rilla? Beth?'

For a few moments no one did or said anything. The entire bush seemed to be holding its breath.

'Rilla,' Beth cried. 'It's coming!'

Rilla turned her attention back to Beth, breaking out of the twilight zone they'd entered. She looked down in dismay to find that Beth was right. The head was right there. *Great!*

She turned to look at Luca. There were seven years of silence and a jumbo load of baggage between them, but Rilla knew that they were in the worst possible place if the baby or Beth needed any emergency care. And estranged husband or not, Luca was an emergency medicine consultant—she wasn't about to look a gift horse in the mouth. She could ponder the fickle finger of fate later.

She swallowed. 'Luca, get down here. I need you.'

Luca knew she hadn't meant *need* him need him, but it didn't stop the quick flare of heat he thought had been extinguished long ago. He took a beat to mentally douse the flame before he responded to the obvious urgency of the situation. He moved closer, crouching down on the rug.

'Is she full term?' he asked. His gaze assessed the situation as his medical training came to the fore.

Rilla shook her head. 'Thirty-six weeks.'

Luca nodded. *Only just premature.* And Beth's belly certainly looked a decent size.

'What do you want me to do?' he asked. He knew Rilla was perfectly capable of delivering a baby hell bent on getting out and didn't see any need to take over. Beth was in good hands.

'Just be here.' Things were out of their control and Rilla knew it. Babies that came as fast as Beth's determined little one practically delivered themselves. All she had to do was catch. 'Just in case.'

She could feel his presence looming beside her and felt strangely claustrophobic in the middle of the wide open bush.

On second thoughts... 'Actually, go down the other end and give Beth something to lean against. Reassure her.'

Luca nodded. Good idea. As far away from Rilla as possible. He shifted around behind Beth, settling her back against his stomach in a supported semi-upright position. Her elbows dug into his thighs for leverage.

Luca looked down into Beth's sweaty face purposely evading Rilla's gaze. A fine film of grime had settled into the furrows of her brow as her face grew red from the effort of suppressing the urge to push.

'You're doing well, Beth,' he said, and gave her a gentle smile. 'Let's just keep this bit slow and easy.' He picked up her hand and gave it a squeeze.

'Easy for you to say,' Beth said, gritting her teeth, and Luca laughed.

'She's nearly crowned,' Rilla said to Beth.

He glanced up, despite telling himself he wouldn't, and caught Rilla's gaze. She was on her knees, her left hand against the baby's head to slow the delivery so Beth wouldn't tear. And she was just as he remembered. Exactly as she was in his dreams.

Her hair was just as thick. As dark and rich as expensive chocolate, and the weight of it in his palms was still almost tangible seven years later. Her long fringe was plastered to her puckered forehead and a hundred memories of sweeping it back while they made love swamped him.

Her eyes were the colour of amber—tawny in some lights, like liquid gold in others. The large freckle that adorned the corner of her mouth like an old fashioned beauty spot, the only blemish on her flawless olive skin, drew his gaze like a moth to flame. Before he knew it he was staring at her mouth, remembering its softness, its secrets.

Luca bit down on a frustrated oath. How the hell had he ended up helping to deliver a baby with his estranged wife in the middle of nowhere? His analytical mind spun at the odds of stumbling across this particular set of sisters on an out-of-the-way bush track. He'd only been back in Brisbane for two days. What kind of sick cosmic joke was this?

But how much more ironic, more cruel was it that a baby was being born as well? The very thing that had been the catalyst that had driven them away from each other seven years ago was the very thing that had now brought them back together for the first time since.

Beth groaned and brought him back to the present. 'You're doing well, Beth,' he soothed quietly, returning his attention to Beth. 'You're so close—isn't she, Rilla?' he added as Beth started to protest.

Rilla swallowed at the familiar way he purred her name, his accent rolling it across his tongue, branding it with his own special stamp of possession. 'Y-yes,' she said huskily.

A couple of voices from behind split the air at that moment and Luca was relieved to see a young couple approaching.

'Have either of you got a mobile phone?' he called, his voice firm and commanding, gaining their attention immediately.

The couple nodded, looking at him uncertainly. 'Yes, but there's no reception,' the woman said.

Luca nodded. 'We know. I need you to run back to the car park and ring for an ambulance. Tell them we've got an imminent delivery of a four-week-premature baby.'

The couple stared for a moment, not moving. 'Now, damn it! Hurry!' Luca demanded. And then Beth cried out again and the couple needed no further encouragement, rushing away.

Beth quietened and Luca searched for some distracting conversation. 'I didn't know you were pregnant, Beth.'

Rilla suppressed a snort. 'Well, you wouldn't. Would you?'

He heard the accusation in her tone and their gazes locked, hers flashing rich gold embers. *Had she cared?* He'd left the country with the distinct impression she never wanted to see him ever again. He noticed her ring finger was minus the gold band he'd given her, and he wondered how long she'd waited before removing it.

Beth moaned, interrupting the sudden tension. The moan turned into a full-throated roar as her birth canal stretched unbearably to accommodate the baby's head. Rilla talked calmly over the top of her.

'OK, Bethy, just pant now. The head's crowning. Pant through it,' Rilla instructed.

'I…can't,' Beth yelled.

Rilla knew that the urge to expel the baby was now a biological imperative and that all women got to a point where they felt defeated.

'Yes, you can,' Rilla and Luca chorused, then glanced at each other, startled by their synchronicity.

'Like this.' Luca demonstrated through the ruckus Beth was kicking up. He panted like a shaggy dog in a heat wave.

Rilla felt a spike of insane jealousy as Luca coaxed Beth through the last gruelling part of the birth. This was the Luca she knew. The Luca she'd loved. The consummate professional whose rapport with people was legendary.

Was this how he would have been had she carried their baby to term? Would he have held her hand and panted with her and looked at her like she was performing the most amazing miracle on earth?

The irony of the situation smacked her in the face. Kneeling on the ground, witnessing the wonder of new life, had brought all their old problems into sharp focus. Her sister was giving birth. The thing she hadn't managed to do and in not doing so had driven a wedge so deeply between them they hadn't been able to find a way back to each other.

Beth cried out and Rilla murmured words of encouragement. She looked at Luca's downcast head. This could have been her, here with Luca.

The constant emptiness that gnawed away at her womb returned with ferocious intent. She'd give anything to be in Beth's position now, an attentive Luca by her side, about to hold his baby in her arms.

She'd felt the loss of their baby so acutely the past couple of years, more so during her sister's pregnancy. And being here with Beth, sharing this experience with Luca, was so bitter-sweet she wanted to cry.

'OK, here she comes,' Rilla announced, keeping her hand against the baby's head as it inexorably eased out. 'Nearly there, Beth,' she encouraged. 'Keep panting.'

'This is it,' Luca agreed, dropping a kiss on Beth's brow and rubbing his hands up and down her arms.

The action distracted Rilla and her gaze was drawn to his wedding band still firmly in place. She blinked. *He still wore it?* After all this time? She'd have bet money on him removing it as soon as he'd left the country. Maybe she wasn't the only sentimental fool?

Beth cried out and Rilla returned her attention to the situation. Seconds later her niece's head slowly emerged into Rilla's waiting hands.

'You did it, you did it.' Rilla beamed as she automatically inserted her fingers to check for the cord, her skills more innate than she'd realised.

'Oh God, is it over?' Beth panted, collapsing hard against Luca.

'Just the shoulders now,' Rilla assured her as her fingers found the one thing she didn't want to—thick, slippery rope wrapped around the baby's neck.

'Oh, no,' she whispered, lifting her gaze to Luca's.

Luca saw the streak of fear flash like lightning through the tawny embers of her eyes. 'What?'

Rilla's pulse slowed and then stopped before stuttering to life in a frantic rhythm. 'The cord…'

Every scrap of medical knowledge she'd ever learned seeped from her brain as blind panic took hold. Her niece had the umbilical cord wrapped around her neck.

Wrapped around her neck. Around her neck.

A thousand worst-case scenarios stomped through her mind like a pack of rampaging rhinos. Luckily Beth was completely oblivious, still caught up in post-head delivery euphoria. She looked at Luca, her mind chaotic.

'It's OK, Rilla.' Luca smiled at her, his gaze brimming with confidence. 'Just pull it over the head. You'll be fine.'

Rilla stared at him, his calm gaze slicing through the escalating horror. He nodded at her and she pulled herself back from the tight grasp of panic and nodded back.

'What's happening?' Beth asked. 'Why do I still have half a baby stuck in me?'

Rilla's hand trembled as she methodically pulled the cord over her niece's head. Luckily it was only wrapped around once. 'Nothing,' she said, and smiled gratefully, mouthing, 'Thank you,' to Luca.

Luca inclined his head slightly and smiled back. 'Give another push now, Beth, and the baby will be out,' he encouraged.

Rilla felt goose-bumps wash over her and marvelled at how a few calm words from Luca had pulled her back from the edge. As shocking as it was to see him here today, she thanked the fates for sending him. Would she have coped if he hadn't been here, hadn't believed in her?

Beth nodded. 'I hope so,' she panted, as she braced herself to bear down again.

Rilla caught the body as it slipped out and the little girl didn't even wait a second to let out an indignant cry, her fists waving in the air. Rilla laughed, relieved after her earlier fright to be holding the annoyed newborn. She passed the baby to an eager Beth.

'Congratulations.' Luca smiled, giving the baby a quick surreptitious once-over, performing a mental APGAR score, satisfied after the cord problem to see she was pink, with a very healthy set of lungs. 'You've given birth to a very angry young lady.'

Beth laughed and then burst into tears as her

precious, naked, bawling daughter was placed in her arms. 'Look, Ril, look,' she cried. 'Isn't she the most beautiful thing you've ever seen?'

Rilla nodded, a lump in her throat the size of an iceberg as she hugged Beth and gazed down into the red, scrunched-up, angry face of her niece. 'She is.'

Luca saw the tears in Rilla's eyes and was irresistibly drawn to her. Her face was sweaty and her hair was messy and she had a smudge of dirt on her cheek but she was looking at her niece like she was the most precious thing in the entire world and he couldn't remember a time when she'd looked more beautiful.

It certainly hadn't been the way he'd imagined he'd meet her again. Of the thousand scenarios that had formed in his head, this hadn't been one of them. He'd hoped for a much more controlled setting. Somewhere removed from their memories, from their shared past. Hopefully in the politically correct surroundings of work.

This was…wild. Primitive. Full of raw human emotion and as such it was impossible to not feel connected to her and all they had been. He looked down at the still bawling newborn. Beth and Rilla were huddled together, laughing and talking at her. Rilla was stroking the infant's head.

No. He hadn't been prepared for this touching, emotionally charged situation.

He'd spent the last seven years buried in his work, trying to forget the mess he'd made with Rilla. Two years back in Italy, licking his wounds, and the next five in London, working his butt off. Losing their baby and their marriage falling apart had hurt so much he'd sworn he was never going to put himself through it again. He wouldn't allow a vision of Rilla and her niece to derail his purpose after less than an hour.

A distant siren broke his train of thought and he was thankful for the reprieve from memory lane. He hadn't come back here for her. He'd come back for closure. To prove to himself he was over her. So he could sign the papers and get on with his life.

'Right. Come on, ladies, let's get this show on the road.' The baby seemed perfectly healthy but he knew the hospital would want to check her out very closely due to her prematurity and rather unorthodox arrival. He took his shirt off and held it out so they could wrap the baby in it.

He stood. 'Rilla, take the baby.' He didn't look at her, just waited for Beth to pass the baby over. Then he picked Beth up, bringing the rug with him and effectively cocooning her. 'Your ambulance awaits,' he said, grinning down at Beth.

'You can't carry me, Luca,' Beth protested as she hung on to his neck.

'Of course I can,' he said cheerfully as he headed towards the ever-louder siren. 'Hold on. It's not far now.'

Rilla was given no choice but to follow as her niece was still connected to her mother via the umbilical cord. Luca's strong naked back and powerful stride bobbed before her with each footfall. His physique was as magnificent as she remembered, and if she hadn't had to watch her step with her precious cargo, the ripple of the muscles in his broad shoulders would have been completely entrancing.

Her niece squirmed in her arms, demanding

attention as if she knew her aunt was distracted. The baby seemed tiny, swallowed up in the folds of Luca's big shirt, and his fragrance wafted temptingly towards her. Myriad memories involving Luca wearing nothing but his cologne almost caused her to stumble.

Her hands tightened around her niece. *This wouldn't do.* Dr Luca Romano had been hers...once. But that had been eight long years ago and she was finally moving on with her life.

Even if his back still looked as good and he still smelled divine and he'd helped deliver her niece. Seven years of silence bred a lot of discontent. And she was never going there again.

CHAPTER TWO

RILLA tried to ignore the betraying flutter of her heart as she waited for the imminent arrival of Dr Luca Romano. It had been ten days since the birth of her niece. Ten days of knowing he was back, of expecting to look over her shoulder and see him. Beth had told her he'd popped in to see the baby every day during their admission, so she knew he'd been at the General. But he'd made no attempt to contact her, which only made this moment even bigger.

The place was abuzz with speculation about the new director of emergency. Few people in the department had been around long enough to remember him from eight years ago. Or, thanks to her insistence she keep her maiden name, to know that once upon a time he and Rilla had been married.

She figured it wouldn't take long though, the hospital grapevine what it was.

'You going to be OK, Rilla?' Julia Woods, the NUM asked, sidling up to her.

Rilla forced a smile to her lips as she carried out the daily task of checking the resus trolley, pleased to have the routine. 'Of course,' she dismissed.

'I'm sorry, he had some admin stuff to attend to so he thought it would be a good opportunity to drop in and meet everyone informally before he started next week. I could hardly say no.'

'Of course,' Rilla replied.

'Have you seen him since he's been back in the country?'

Rilla shut her eyes briefly, the image of his naked back as he strode along the track with Beth in true hero fashion burnt into her retinas. 'Yes,' she said noncommittally, her hand shaking slightly as she checked the light on the laryngoscope. 'It'll be fine, Julia. Really.'

Rilla saw the doubt in her boss's gaze. Julia had known her for a long time. Had gone to their wedding. She knew how hard the separation and the intervening years had been on Rilla.

'Really,' Rilla reassured her, giving Julia's arm a quick squeeze.

An hour later all the nursing staff were summoned to the staffroom to meet the new director. Rilla contemplated not going. It wasn't like she needed an introduction. And if they'd been busy she would have stayed behind to man the fort, but the post-night duty lull was in full swing and unless a disaster struck, it would probably be another hour before today's patients start tricking through the doors.

And then there was the message that not going would send. To those who knew their history. And to Luca. It was going to be hard enough working together again without people's pity. It was time to show everyone, including Luca, that she was over him and moving on with her life.

As far as work was concerned, her baggage with Luca was in the past. Once word got out of their prior relationship they would be watched and speculated over endlessly. Rilla had to start on the right foot. Had to project an it's-OK, it's-all-in-the-past, the-divorce-papers-are-out-there, we've-moved-on aura. Even if it killed her.

Still, as he entered the staffroom, she wasn't prepared for the sight of him. On Friday, due to the urgency of the situation, she hadn't paid much attention to his attire, apart from when he'd been shirtless. But today, dressed in his work clothes, he looked devastatingly hand-some. Like the old Luca.

His dark trousers sat low on his hips, the pleats at his waistband pressed perfectly, sitting in a way that emphasised the narrowness of his hips. His crisp navy blue business shirt was luxuriously thick. His zigzag-patterned tie classy.

So much for a casual meet and greet.

She didn't have to check his clothing labels to know they were Italian, as were his soft black leather shoes. Luca had always dressed with complete and utter class. His wardrobe had had more labels than hers and she had teased him unmercilessly about it when they had first got together.

But it was about more than the designer quality

of his clothes. It was how he wore them. He'd always exuded charisma but now there was supreme confidence. Arrogance, almost. Once she would have put it down to his Italian roots or his noble Latin features, but she wasn't so sure any more.

There was a distance to his demeanour, a streak of aloofness that moulded his raw sex appeal into something much more mature, more dangerous. And she didn't think it had anything to do with ancestry. Whatever it was, the combination was powerful. Luca Romano was still a pleasure to watch.

Rilla was pleased to note, though, that there was some evidence of ageing. It hadn't just been her. At thirty-five his black hair had some grey streaks. It looked more severe too. The length had been tamed. It had once brushed his collar and flopped a little in his eyes. Now it was more closely cropped. But it only succeeded in drawing attention to his amazing fringe of thick sooty lashes.

The few extra lines around his eyes and mouth in no way marred his handsome face. His jaw was just as square, his nose as patrician. He was still tall and lean and most definitely wearing his years well.

Rilla could see the fact was not lost on some of the younger nurses and was surprised by the hot shaft of jealousy that sliced through her. It shouldn't have. Luca had, after all, always aroused this kind of reaction in women. Once, secure in his love, she'd taken pride in it, knowing he had been hers. Now it was as irritating as hell.

There were ten nursing staff on the morning shift and Julia introduced each one. Luca was his usual charming self. Not hurried. Taking the time to ask each one about themselves, putting everyone at ease, making them laugh. He was a hit.

'Of course, you know Rilla,' Julia said as she came to her second-in-charge.

'Of course,' Luca said, inclining his head.

They locked gazes for a moment, his accent sliding over her skin, eight years of history thick between them. Rilla felt her cheeks grow warm as Luca's gaze moved quickly on to the next person, excruciatingly aware of the curious stares of her in-the-know colleagues.

She was pleased to escape ten minutes later after Luca's brief new-broom speech finished with a my-door-is-always-open assurance. But his gaze was careful not to encompass her and she got the distinct impression she wasn't included.

By midmorning the lull was well and truly over. In fact, the department had descended into bedlam. Ambulances arrived with frightening regularity, unloading their cargo of car-accident victims, asthmatics and chest pain sufferers, filling the resus bays.

The usual suspects swelled the waiting room out front with a mishmash of legitimate illnesses and minor time-consuming complaints—sore throats, vague pains, migraines, fevers, paper cuts.

The combined noise could have given a crowded theatre before curtain-up a run for its money. Not that Rilla noticed, well used to the low-level chaos that the emergency department became most days. And today, after the unsettling brush with Luca, she was more than grateful for the background hum distracting her from buried memories, newly roused.

Just before lunch the appropriately nicknamed Bat-phone rang. It was red and their direct link to the ambulance control centre. Rilla took the call about the imminent code-one arrival of a ten-day-old baby with apnoea. She replaced the receiver, a sudden chill up her spine as her thoughts instantly turned to her ten-day-old niece.

How worried the parents must be that their baby was having episodes where it stopped breathing. She quickly sorted through the possible causes. A seizure? Maybe caused by a brain infection or cranial trauma from an accidental or non-accidental injury. A respiratory infection? A near cot death?

'Apnoeic ten-day-old. ETA two minutes,' Rilla told Henry Bosch, the junior resident, as she entered the resus cubicles to prepare the area.

Henry gave her a startled look and Rilla could see the convulsive bob of his Adam's apple.

'Where's Karen?' he asked.

Rilla wished the senior reg was there too as she recognised the wail of a distant siren. 'She's still up with Julie and the resus team, dealing with the arrest on ward eleven. I've paged her. You're it until then.' Rilla smiled and injected confidence into her voice.

Please, let this kid be fine by the time it gets here.

There was no more time for wishes as the siren blared louder, announcing its arrival outside. 'Let's hustle,' she said to Henry.

The ambulance doors opened and Rilla's worst fears were confirmed when she saw the paramedic huddled over a small form, ambu-bag in place over the tiny face.

'Ten-day-old baby, four weeks prem, three-day history of upper respiratory tract infection, Mum has a cold.' The paramedic rattled off a brisk, succinct handover, eyes not leaving the baby as his partner slowly pulled the gurney from the car.

Sounds like an RSV picture, Rilla thought. The respiratory virus could affect babies very seriously, making them desperately ill. Especially if there was a history of prematurity.

'Lethargic and poor feeding today. Mum had babe at the GP when she had a prolonged apnoea, resolving with stimulation. GP called the ambulance. Three further episodes en route, requiring vigorous stimulation and oxygen therapy.'

'Rilla!'

Rilla turned, startled by the hysterical call, shocked to see Beth getting out of the passenger side of the ambulance.

'Beth?' Rilla gasped, looking at her sister's tear- stained, frantic face. 'What the…?' She swivelled her head back to the tiny baby on the gurney, looking small and defenceless on the huge trolley. Bridie? Beth reached her and Rilla enfolded her distraught sister in her arms, her heart hammering madly as her sluggish brain connected the dots. This apnoeic, seriously ill baby was her niece?

'It's all my fault,' Beth sobbed. 'I gave her my cold. Her lungs are too premature to cope with it. Oh, my God, I don't want her to die.'

Rilla would have given anything at that moment to be in possession of a magic wand.

Anything. Instead, she was it. The only senior nurse they had around until Julia got back from the arrest, and she had only a very junior doctor at her disposal.

Her brain raced as she prioritised. 'Bridie's going to be fine, just fine,' Rilla soothed as she hurried inside, dragging Beth with her, keeping up with the gurney. 'You know she's in the best hands here,' she said, 'the best.'

Rilla prayed to every god she could think of plus the ones she couldn't, that she was right. She froze out the sickening worry of an aunt and the more basic pull of sisterhood. She had to remove herself emotionally from her tiny niece, struggling to breathe, and her frantic sister.

'You're going to have to intubate,' Rilla told Henry briskly as she hooked Bridie up to the monitors and another apnoea required Rilla to give a vigorous sternal rub before it resolved. This time Bridie's heart rate slowed and her oxygen saturations dipped. The situation was worsening.

'We need to secure her airway,' Rilla said, ignoring the frantic beat of her heart as she handed the laryngoscope, endotracheal tube and other equipment to Henry. One of the junior nurses was drawing up some intubation drugs.

'Brenda, go put out a code blue page,' Rilla ordered as Henry prepared to intubate. His hand shook and Rilla had the awful feeling he was going to foul it up.

Intubating a child or baby was always a little fraught, but in an emergency and for the first time? She knew Henry had to be feeling the pressure. Better to get as many medical people as possible down here so someone more experienced could take over. Hell, she'd ring the chief of staff, if she had to. Her father may not have had recent clinical experience but she'd bet her last cent he could intubate Bridie with his eyes closed.

Beth was crying and clutching at Rilla's uniform, begging them both to do something as alarms shrilled all around them. Damn it! Rilla felt like her heart was being torn in two. She wanted to be over there comforting Beth but Bridie needed her too. At this moment even more than her sister.

'Did you notify Gabe?' Rilla asked as she administered the muscle-paralysis drug so Henry could pass the tube through Bridie's vocal cords.

'I paged him. He's in Theatre. He didn't want to go in today,' Beth cried. 'But he was fussing so much and it was only a short list. She wasn't that bad this morning. I shouldn't have made him go,' she wailed.

'It's OK, Beth,' Rilla assured her, her pulse rate sky-rocketing as Henry attempted to insert the endotracheal tube. 'I'll send someone for him, I promise. Let's just do this first, OK? It's going to be fine. Nearly done.'

Only Rilla knew it wasn't. Knew Henry was having trouble, and as she saw Bridie's saturations plummet and her heart rate drop, she knew he was going to have to stop, re-oxygenate and try again.

'Do you want me to give some atropine?' she prompted Henry, and gave it when he nodded.

'Oh God,' Beth cried.

Where was the team? It seemed like an hour but in reality it had only been a minute. Satisfied that Bridie's heart rate had stabilised and that Henry had control of the airway, Rilla made a decision.

'I'll be back in two seconds,' she announced.

'Ril, no! Where are you going?' Beth demanded, her voice raising several octaves.

Rilla turned and looked at her sister. She grabbed her arms and gave them a gentle squeeze. 'I'm going to call Dad.'

Beth's face crumpled. 'OK.'

Rilla paced out of the resus area into the corridor. Taking a couple of deep cleansing breaths, her hands shaking, she headed for the nearest phone. Before she could pick it up, her gaze met Luca's.

'Rilla? What's wrong,' he demanded, striding towards her. She looked like hell. Pale and shaken and about two seconds away from collapsing.

'Luca. Thank God,' Rilla said, putting her hand out to steady herself on his outstretched arm. She knew he wasn't officially at work yet but she didn't care. Bridie's life depended on him. She'd never been more pleased to see him. Not even in the bush ten days ago. 'I need you. It's Bridie.'

Luca didn't ask any questions, just followed her brisk lead. He listened as she prattled off the details and he swore under his breath as his sharp gaze took in the situation in the resus area.

'Luca,' Beth sobbed. 'Oh, Luca.'

Luca gave Beth's hands a brief squeeze before muscling a relieved Henry aside and with Rilla's assistance slid the endotracheal tube past the vocal cords and into the trachea in one smooth movement.

'It's OK now, Beth,' Luca soothed, as he held the tube with one hand and bagged with the other while Rilla, hands still shaking, secured the tube with brown tape. 'She's going to be OK. We won't let anything happen to our little bush baby.'

Julia and Karen arrived in the resus bay, along with a PICU consultant, just as Rilla was satisfied the tube was secure. Luca and Henry filled in the details and Rilla was pleased to let them take over so she could comfort her sister. So she could be a worried aunt.

'Come on out with me,' Rilla encouraged. 'Bridie's in good hands. She'll be up in ICU before you know it.'

'No,' Beth shook her head vigorously, wiping at her eyes with her hands. 'I can't leave her.'

Rilla nodded, knowing if it was her baby she wouldn't be able to either. 'I'll ring Dad. We'll get him to go and talk to Gabe.'

'Oh God, Gabe.' Beth dissolved into more tears.

'Shush,' Rilla soothed, rubbing Beth's arm. 'He'll be here soon.'

Rilla didn't even get three paces out of the resus bay before the enormity of the situation overwhelmed her. She groped for a nearby wall and sagged against it. Her breath hurt in her chest and tears stung her eyes as visions of her niece's still body and pale lips replayed in her head. The what-ifs were crippling.

'Rilla?'

She looked up to find Luca standing in front of her, his gaze gentle, a frown marring his forehead. She sucked in some much-needed air.

'Are you OK, *cara*?'

Rilla nodded her head vigorously as his quiet endearment brought her perilously close to breaking down. She breathed in and out a few more times, grabbing at the sharp pain in her side. 'I'll be OK.' Her voice was shaky and she knew it. 'I was just… It was just…'

Luca nodded. She didn't have to explain. 'I know.'

They looked at each other for a few seconds. 'I don't know how to thank you. You've come to the rescue twice now with Bridie.'

Luca shrugged. 'She's my niece too.'

Rilla felt her eyes widen, a storm of emotions battering her already precarious state. Did he think he could waltz back in after all this time and play happy families with her? Why was he here? What did he want? Damn him! She didn't have time for this now.

'I…I have to call my father.'

He nodded. 'You sure you'll be OK?'

Rilla nodded back.

'I'll go and check how things are going.'

When Rilla re-entered Resus a few minutes later, Luca was holding a sobbing Beth and Rilla's heart did a triple back somersault with a twist. He looked so big and manly, stroking her sister's head. So like the old Luca. The one she'd fallen in love with. Not like the distant, worka-holic stranger he'd become after the miscarriage.

'Dad's finding Gabe,' Rilla said as she approached.

'Oh, thank you,' Beth said, her voice strained with emotion. 'Look at me.' Beth blew her nose. 'I must be such a mess. So much for the capable nurse. I just fell apart.'

'Of course you did,' Rilla soothed. 'She's your baby.'

'They think it's RSV,' Beth said, her voice thick with emotion and the remnants of her cold. 'They say she'll be tu-tubed for a few days.' Beth broke down again and this time sought comfort in her sister's arms.

'Beth?'

Rilla looked up to find her father and an ashen-faced Gabe, still in his scrubs, staring at his daughter, who looked increasingly small amongst all the medical equipment that Julia, Karen and the ICU doctor and nurse kept adding. Beth ran straight into his arms, sobbing loudly. 'I'm so sorry, Gabe. It all happened so fast.'

'Shh,' he soothed. 'She's in good hands now.'

'How are you, darling?'

John Winters embraced his middle daughter.

'I've been better.' Rilla hugged her father. 'Thank goodness for Luca being around. He was...' her eyes met Luca's over her father's shoulder '...magnificent.'

It was true. He'd been calm and focused under pressure. He'd been exactly what Bridie had needed. What she'd needed—again. Their gazes locked.

John moved out of Rilla's embrace and shook his son-in-law's hand. 'Thank you, Luca. Again.'

Minutes later Bridie was attached to the transport ventilator and was ready to move up to PICU.

'Julia, I know we're frantic but—'

'Go,' Julia ordered Rilla with a dismissive wave of her hand. 'Of course you must go. Don't worry about us. We'll be fine. Just look after that niece of yours. And your sister.'

Rilla gave her boss a hug. Deserting her post on a frantic day was not going to win any brownie points for the NUM job but it was moments like these that put trifling things like jobs firmly into perspective, and Julia understood that family came first. It was why she was leaving her beloved post, uprooting her kids and following her husband and his new job to Canada.

Luca accompanied them, down corridors and up lifts, walking silently beside Rilla. Ahead Gabe and Beth huddled together, seeking comfort and support from each other and Rilla yearned to be able to do the same with Luca. She was so worried about Bridie, she could feel a knot in the pit of her stomach the size of a cricket ball and her legs felt like a dubious support. Once she would have leant on Luca automatically. But so much had changed.

The ICU nurse asked them all to wait in the parents' lounge, promising to get them as soon as they had Bridie settled.

'You don't have to stay,' Rilla said quietly as Luca took a seat next to her. He'd removed his tie and undone the top two buttons and she quashed the stupid urge to crawl onto his lap.

He turned and looked at her. 'I'm staying.'

Rilla swallowed, absurdly happy by his insistence. She shouldn't be. She should be angry.

Why hadn't he offered this level of support when she'd needed it seven years ago? Instead, he had thrown himself into his work, grown away from her. *As had she.* Too ill equipped to deal with the tragic end to a fledgling pregnancy so early in their relationship.

But he was here now, all solid and silent and dependable, and as confusing as it was, she'd take it for the moment. Because Bridie was by no means out of the woods and Luca had always made her feel like she could cope with anything when he was by her side. Well, for a while, anyway.

An increasingly fretting Beth and Gabe were ushered inside twenty minutes later. Given that they were all on staff at the hospital and the patient was the chief of staff's granddaughter, the unit's policy of only two visitors at a time could no doubt have been bent, but Rilla knew her sister and brother-in-law needed time by themselves with Bridie.

A frantic Hailey arrived, followed closely by Penny Winters.

'Darling. What happened? How is she? Oh, poor Beth,' Penny gabbled.

John embraced his wife. 'She's ventilated. They think she has a respiratory infection. We don't know much more than that at the moment.'

Penny held her arms out to her daughters and Rilla and Hailey embraced their mother. 'She'll be fine, Mum,' Rilla assured her.

'Has anyone contacted David?' Hailey asked.

They all looked at each other. 'Damn! No.' John shook his head and flipped open his mobile phone. 'I'll do it now.'

'David?' Luca murmured to Rilla as he watched John leave the room.

'Beth's son.'

Luca frowned. 'The one she put up for adoption when she was fifteen? Just before your parents fostered her?'

Rilla nodded, not surprised that he'd remembered. He had been very close to her family. 'He found her earlier this year.'

'That's wonderful,' Luca enthused quietly. 'Beth must have been ecstatic.'

Rilla swallowed a lump, thinking about all the things he'd missed out on. The things they could have shared, that he could have been part of. 'She was.'

Another hour passed while the family waited. The television was on in the background, a welcome distraction, but no one could really concentrate on it for any length of time. They made idle chit-chat, all the time on tenterhooks.

Luca looked at his watch. It was two o'clock. He saw the strain and felt the tension in the room and felt as helpless as the rest of the Winters family. Whether he wanted it or not, he and Bridie were connected.

And not just because she was his estranged wife's niece but because he'd been at her birth. Had put a tube in her throat today to save her life. After seven years of silence he wasn't sure if he belonged here any more, amongst this shocked family, but he felt compelled to stay anyway.

Not just for him but for Rilla. OK, he'd come back to give himself some closure, to prove he was over her and sign the divorce papers, but

Rilla was in the midst of a crisis and nothing else mattered for the moment other than Bridie getting well.

'I'm going to go and get us all some lunch,' he announced, standing and stretching.

He returned fifteen minutes later with a variety of prepackaged sandwiches, muffins, chocolate bars and a tray full of cappuccinos. Gabe entered the room as the food was being devoured. They all stood.

'How is she?' John asked.

'Her condition is still unstable. Her blood gases are terrible and they keep escalating her ventilation. They've had to keep her paralysed to ventilate her adequately.'

Gabe's voice cracked and they all crowded closer, touching his arm, rubbing his back and hugging him.

'How's Beth?' Luca asked.

Gabe rubbed his eyes. 'Terrible. She's exhausted. Bridie hasn't been sleeping or feeding well the last few nights because of the cold, so Beth's pretty sleep deprived on top of being scared out of her mind.'

'Has she eaten?' Rilla asked.

Gabe shook his head. 'I've tried to persuade her to come out and have some lunch but she's adamant she's fine.'

'Right.' Rilla nodded. 'You sit and have something to eat and I'll see if I can persuade her. Bossy sister might work better.'

Gabe nodded. 'Thank you.'

Rilla was stopped at the door by Luca's. 'Do you want company?'

She looked back over her shoulder. The thought of seeing Bridie so ill was sickening and she was surprised at how very, very much she did want Luca with her. 'Two at a time. That's the rules,' she pointed out.

'Forget the rules,' Luca said, striding towards her.

They spoke briefly with the ICU doctor who had helped earlier before going into Bridie's isolation room. Beth looked dreadful, her face puffy, her hair rumpled. Rilla hugged her and Beth's face crumpled.

'She's getting worse,' she sobbed into Rilla's shoulder.

'Shh,' Rilla crooned. 'The doctor was just saying they've confirmed it's RSV. You know they always get worse before they get better.'

Rilla looked at her niece lying in the warming cot, wires criss-crossing her tiny body like railway tracks. The monitor displayed multi-coloured squiggles representing heart rate and blood pressure as well as respiratory rate and oxygen saturations.

Bridie had only been two and half kilos at birth and the illness had set her weight gain back. She was so pale, her legs slightly mottled. She looked lifeless and Rilla could see why Beth was so distraught.

Rilla stroked Bridie's fingers, which were just sticking out from beneath some bandages. An IV line had been placed in her arm and it had been bundled up to keep it secure.

'Hey sweetie,' she crooned, 'your Aunty Ril's here. We all are.'

She looked over her shoulder at Luca. She was conscious of his presence behind her and his quick reassuring smile bolstered her flagging confidence that everything would be all right. He placed a hand on her shoulder and his thumb stroked the tense muscles of her neck.

'Beth, Luca bought some lunch. Why don't you come outside and have something to eat?'

Beth shook her head vigorously.

'You need to keep your strength up, Beth,' Rilla cajoled.

'I can't leave her.' Beth shook her head again.

Rilla could see the determined jut of her sister's chin. She needed to eat. She looked like she was ready to drop. Rilla despaired that she wouldn't find the right words and she looked up at Luca. He squeezed her shoulder and mouthed, 'Let me.'

'Beth,' Luca said, coming around to kneel beside her. 'You need to look after yourself. Bridie is in the best place, being looked after by the best people. You need to rest and eat and drink regularly. They're going to want you to start expressing milk soon to provide Bridie with much-needed calories to help her recover quickly. Your milk supply will suffer if you don't take care of yourself. You wouldn't want that, would you?'

Beth raised her face to look at Luca. 'No,' she sniffled.

'OK, then. I promise Rilla and I will stay here right by her side until you get back. We won't leave her, will we, Rilla?'

Rilla felt mesmerised by his low, accented voice. His sincerity was strangely seductive. 'No. Absolutely not.'

Beth looked at Rilla then back at Luca. 'OK. But just for a short while.'

'Of course,' Rilla said.

And that set up the pattern for the next two nights and days. As the medical team supported Bridie, adjusting to each phase of the illness, the family rallied to make sure that Beth and Gabe were getting enough rest and time away and looking after themselves.

Penny cooked nutritious meals and tempting snacks, feeding them all as they maintained their vigil at the hospital, grabbing brief moments of sleep where they could along with quick showers and hasty clothing changes.

Rilla didn't leave the hospital at all, the vision of Bridie the day she'd come in by ambulance still too fresh in her mind. Luca stayed by her side and was a huge support for the entire family, volunteering to do the myriad things that needed doing outside the hospital so the family could stay together.

And, of course, when it was her turn to be with Bridie—night or day—he was by her side. It was odd, spending so much time in his company after seven years of no contact at all. By tacit agreement they didn't talk about their own issues, even though she kept asking herself why. Why was he back? Why was he acting like he was still a part of the Winters clan? Like he still wanted to be part?

For the moment it was immensely comforting to have Luca with her. Their time for questions would come soon enough.

'So how did Gabe and Beth meet?' Luca asked as they sat beside Bridie in the wee small hours of the third day.

He'd been watching Rilla for the last hour as she'd struggled to keep her eyes open, the tawny flecks in her amber eyes visible even in the subdued light of the room. He remembered numerous times when she'd looked at him with slumberous eyes, turning in his arms and snuggling against him, her head beneath his chin as she'd fallen asleep.

'The Fisher twins,' Rilla said, rousing herself from the thick web of exhaustion. She'd had maybe ten hours of sleep in small blocks over the last couple of days and it was catching up with her.

Luca frowned. 'The conjoined twins?' Luca recalled the case instantly. There had been a lot of global press and he'd paid particular attention because of the connection with his old hospital, the Brisbane General.

Rilla nodded. 'Gabe was the surgeon who separated them. Beth is NUM of operating theatres here. They worked very closely on the case. Bridie's named after one of the twins.'

Luca had always had a soft spot for Rilla's older sister. 'I'm pleased Beth got her happily-ever-after. She's had a tough life, she deserves it.'

Rilla agreed. Beth had been through a lot before the Winters family had taken her in, and no one was more worthy of happiness.

But what about me? About us?

Rilla didn't know where the errant thought came from. Maybe it was the hour, maybe it was the persistent tug of tiredness, but the urge to demand answers was suddenly overwhelming.

Bridie coughed and the ventilator alarm was triggered, along with the monitor, and the words died on her lips. *This is not the place, Rilla. Not the place.* Concentrate on Bridie and worry about Luca and his motives another time.

Later that morning they had their first piece of good news. Ventilation had been reduced. Bridie's condition was stabilising. She'd turned the corner.

Beth was over the moon. It was the first time Rilla had seen her sister smile in three days. Everyone was kissing and hugging each other, and Rilla was so relieved that when Luca kissed her she kissed him back enthusiastically. 'Isn't it great?' she enthused, pulling away. A shot of adrenaline charged through her system. She wasn't entirely sure it had anything to do with her niece's improved condition either.

'It's the best,' Luca agreed, savouring the taste of her after seven years of famine.

Bridie improved rapidly over the course of the day and the medical staff were hoping to have her extubated by tomorrow or the next day at the latest. The mood was suddenly lighter. Their collective tiredness magically evaporated.

Beth and Gabe ordered everyone home later that night.

'Now we know she's turned the corner, we're going to sleep in the parents' lounge tonight on one of the pull-out sofas,' Beth said. 'We're both exhausted. So are all of you. We can't thank you enough for all the support these last few days but you need to go to your homes. Sleep in your beds.'

The family protested and fussed but Beth was adamant and they eventually all agreed they could do with a good night's sleep. Rilla and Luca hung around for a few hours after everyone else had left. She felt too anxious to leave. Her home was furthest away and she wanted to be close should Bridie relapse.

'Go home,' Beth ordered at close to midnight as Gabe prepared their sofa bed.

'I don't mind staying the night,' she stalled.

'Luca, take her home,' Beth said, hands on hips.

Luca rose and Rilla shot him a 'down, boy' glare. 'But everyone else is so much closer.'

'You're only ten minutes away,' Beth pointed out.

'Mum and Dad and Hailey are two,' Rilla returned.

'So go stay with them.'

'They'll all be asleep by now and I don't have a key any more.' Rilla knew she was going to sleep like the dead. She didn't want to wake any of them from their first decent sleep in three days.

'I'm two minutes away,' Luca interrupted. Why he did so, he had no idea. But it made sense.

Rilla looked at him, startled. She saw Beth look at Gabe in her peripheral vision.

'Problem solved,' Beth said brightly.

'Luca, no,' Rilla said, shying from the intense blackness of his eyes.

'You're tired, I'm tired. I live closer. It's just geography, *cara*.'

'He's right,' Beth pushed.

Rilla looked from one to the other. She knew

he was right. Except he said *'cara'* and she wanted to melt. Rilla wavered.

'You can sleep in the spare room,' Luca said.

Well, she sure as hell wasn't going to be sleeping with him.

'Damn right I will,' she said, gathering her stuff and heading for the door, Luca's sexy chuckle following her.

CHAPTER THREE

RILLA was exhausted. Utterly, deep-down-in-her-bones, one hundred per cent exhausted. But despite the weariness of her body, the charged silence in Luca's car was keeping her super-alert. She must have been crazy to agree to this. There was too much to say, too much to talk about. And she just wasn't up for it. Not tonight.

Luca pulled into the driveway, braked and turned the engine off. She looked at the flat that had been their home for the brief time they'd been together, too shattered to move, memories swamping her. The things they'd gotten up to between those four walls...

She'd moved in with Luca within weeks of meeting him, so in love, so sure of their love. The flat hadn't been much, but they hadn't needed much. Back then, all they'd needed had been each other.

After they'd returned from their Italian honeymoon they'd planned on buying a house and had been actively looking when her bombshell pregnancy had been revealed. Then all their carefully laid plans had gone out the window.

After their marriage had disintegrated she'd moved out and eventually bought herself an apartment at South Bank. Luca had kept the flat, placing it in the hands of a rental agency just prior to leaving the country, and it had been occupied on and off for the past seven years.

Rilla had often found herself in the street, outside the tiny two-bedroom place where they'd first made love. It had become a habit over the years, a bad one, and she'd noticed only last month that the flat was vacant again.

Was she ready to be alone with him? In their little flat full of memories? The attraction was still there, she couldn't deny it. Even after days without sleep, every cell in her body crying out for slumber, it pulsed between them.

Seven years apart hadn't doused the instantaneous flare that heated her body every time she looked at him. If anything, maturity had given him an even sexier edge, stoking the flame higher. And the way he'd stayed by her side had been heroic and appealing on an emotional level that called to her even more than the physical attraction.

'Come on, Rilla,' Luca murmured, breaking the silence in the confines of the car. She was looking at the place as if it were the portal to hell.

She looked at Luca. He looked bigger, darker, sexier in the dimness of the car. Her name rolled off his tongue, accented perfectly, and she shivered.

Oh, God, I'm tired.

'Let's go in,' Luca prompted, leaning forward to unclip her seat belt as she still hadn't made a move. She looked completely done in. Maybe he'd have to carry her? *Please, no.* He wasn't up to such close contact tonight. Her slumberous eyes were already causing his groin to tighten.

'S-sure,' Rilla nodded, sitting very still until he pulled away. Damn it, she wasn't a young woman at the mercy of her hormones any more. She was thirty.

And over him.

Luca opened the door and gestured for her to precede him. He tried and failed not to notice how her button-up red shirt pulled across her generous chest as her arm brushed his. How she was wearing the same perfume she'd worn the night they'd skipped out of the restaurant after entrées and made love for the first time.

Maybe it was the heightened emotional situation with Bridie or his fatigue weakening his resistance, but seven years of denial had come back and smacked him hard in the face. Damn it! He was as hot for her now as he'd ever been. And they were alone. In their flat.

Luca followed her down the short hallway, throwing his keys on the hallstand and ushering her into the lounge room, not even bothering not to look at her hips as they swayed in the A-line skirt she was wearing.

Dio! Give me strength.

He clicked on the lamp and it threw a subtle glow around the room.

'Sit,' he ordered, and escaped to the kitchen, fixing her a cup of tea. He felt the grittiness of his eyes as he waited for the kettle to boil and rubbed the back of his neck, massaging the aching muscles caused from nodding off in horrible, plastic, government-issue chairs.

'I need a shower. Drink this,' he said, holding the mug out to her. 'I won't be long.'

Rilla took it and drank, desperately trying to ignore the fact that Luca, her husband, was wet and naked only metres away.

Estranged husband. Nearly ex-husband.

Still, when Luca strode back into the lounge there was nothing ex about the leap her pulse performed at the sight of his near-nakedness.

'Oh,' Rilla said, her eyes drawn irresistibly to the sheer beauty of his chest.

A thick pelt of dark hair adorned his well-developed pecs and she followed its path as it became sparser, sprinkling lightly across six-pack abs, arrowing down further into a tantalising trail that disappeared behind the undone button of his jeans.

She found herself wondering if he had underwear on or if he'd hastily pulled the jeans on without? The zipper taunted her and she dragged her gaze back to his face with difficulty.

'Finished?' he asked, swallowing hard as he recognised the heat warming the tawny flecks in her eyes.

Luca was used to women looking at him with lust in their eyes but was surprised to discover Rilla was still one of them. There was an annoying twitch in his jeans and he silently cursed himself for his susceptibility.

It had always been like this. Right from the start. Heady and lust-infused. They'd slept together on their third date. And she'd moved in the next week.

'W-what?' Rilla asked, embarrassed to be caught ogling.

'The tea?' Luca pointed at the mug.

Rilla shivered at the way his voice washed over her. His slight accent had always turned her on. In the past he'd whispered to her in Italian as they'd made love and it had always, always taken her over the edge. Even now, after seven years of neglect, his accent stroked across her skin. Heated her belly. Hardened her nipples.

In this house, where every nook and cranny could tell a tale of lust, having Luca standing before her half-naked was a supreme test of her 'over him' theory. She was too emotionally wrung out over Bridie's roller-coaster ride and too tired to resist the innate pull his body had over hers.

She handed the mug back to him as the silence grew between them, and she found herself wishing he would laugh. Throw his head back in that lazy Luca way he had and let forth a deep chuckle that rumbled from his belly and split his handsome face into a sexy grin. Anything to break the tension.

He'd once laughed a lot. They'd both laughed a lot.

She missed him, she realised. *Rather dangerously realised.* The Luca who laughed. And the one who had so often moaned her name. Quivered beneath her touch. Seven years she'd been telling herself she didn't miss him and here, now, in their old flat, she had to face the fact that she'd been lying to herself.

Her tired brain searched for something to say, to regain control. She couldn't afford to let thoughts of yesteryear sweep her away into an alternate reality. They were over. There was no going back.

'I can't believe you came back and didn't even bother to inform me.' She didn't want to get into this with him tonight but her confusion over his motives at least kept him at a distance.

Luca heard the soft accusation in her voice and was pierced by the uncertainty simmering in her amber gaze. Her chest rose and fell in an agitated rhythm, straining the buttons of her shirt. Her dark hair tumbled to her shoulders and two spots of colour stained her cheeks.

How could he still want her after all these years?

Luca sighed and sat beside her on the sofa, throwing his head back into the soft cushion of fabric. Her perfume invaded his personal space and he shut his eyes. 'I knew your father would tell you,' he murmured.

Rilla swivelled her head to look at him. With his eyes closed he looked as weary as she felt.

She shut her eyes too, allowing the quiet of the house to drift her away for a moment.

'I'm sorry. I should have told you.'

Rilla opened her eyes, unsure whether she'd imagined the whispered apology. Luca was staring at her, his dark gaze sleepy and sexy all at once. It was too much and she fluttered her eyes closed again for a few more moments.

She should get up and have a shower. Remove herself from the temptation of his nearness. But it was nice to snuggle into a comfortable sofa and rest her eyes in peace. A thought rose in her foggy brain and she voiced it before it floated away.

'Why did you come back, Luca? To the General? Why not just sign the divorce papers and put an end to something we should never have started in the first place?'

Luca opened his eyes again. Her sleepy gaze was startlingly honest. He shrugged, struggling through the fog of fatigue and lust to remember exactly why he'd been so crazy. 'The divorce papers arrived and I saw the job advertised the next day and I thought, Why not?'

Rilla felt her pulse leap at the mention of the papers. *So he had received them.*

'Time to come back and put the past to rest,' Luca continued. 'And, anyway, it's what I always wanted. We always wanted…remember?'

She did. Vividly. All those hours in bed, spinning their dreams, weaving their futures together. Him, the medical director of the emergency department at the Brisbane General. Her as the NUM. Colleagues and lovers. Partners at work and in life.

'I remember,' she whispered.

His heavy-lidded gaze was mesmerising and Rilla could barely breathe as the air between them was sucked away. She remembered everything about their life together as if it had been yesterday. The laughter, the excitement, the plans, the love. The way everything but them had ceased to exist. They'd been so good together.

Until they'd imploded.

The sinister thought and the memories of that terrible time forced Rilla to sit up straighter. How had they got so close?

'It was a mistake to come.' She rose from the sofa as if she'd been poked with an electric cattle prod. She moved away another step, trying to evade the innate lure that demanded she go closer.

What was the matter with her? Sure, she was emotionally vulnerable and physically over-wrought. But it was no excuse. She wanted to scream at the power he still had over her seven years down the track. But how could she want to scream *and* feel him inside her at the same time?

She could feel the familiar itch under her skin and the prickle in her veins and didn't trust what would happen if she didn't leave immediately.

Theirs had always been a passionate relation-ship. Desire and lust had kept them enthralled, oblivious to all else. A fact that had been driven home to them as the cruel jolt of her miscar-riage had woken them from their haze of lust to discover they hadn't had the wherewithal, the history to make it work.

A lot of water had flowed under the bridge

since then and she was damned if she'd walk that road again. Rilla didn't explain but simply turned around and walked out.

Luca blinked, taking a second to realise she'd gone. *Damn it!* 'Wait,' he called, stalking into the darkened hallway, catching her as she put her hand on the doorknob.

'No,' Rilla threw over her shoulder as she wrenched the door open. She was tired and she wasn't going to do something stupid because neither of them was alert enough to resist. Damn her for her sexual vulnerability and damn him for this insane pull he still had over her.

Luca covered the distance to the doorway in four long strides, placing his hand against the door above her head and pushing it shut, keeping it there, sealing her escape route. 'Stay,' he murmured.

His chest, pressed to her back, crowded her against the doorframe. His other hand automatically went to her hip. They were so close. His breath heaved in his chest. He could smell her perfume and her shampoo. Hear her husky breathing. Her hair was temptingly close, the curve of her neck and the slope of her shoulder visible through the thick chocolate strands.

'Please, *cara*, you said you were going to stay,' he whispered huskily, as his pulse thrilled faster. He moved the hand from her hip to her shoulder and turned her round, pushing against the frame to step back a little, remove himself from the intoxication of her nearness.

Rilla shook her head. 'I haven't got the energy to fight tonight, Luca. To go back over this stuff. I'm tired.'

Their gazes locked for a heat-infused moment. He was too close. Rilla swallowed. The temptation to reach out and touch his jaw was overwhelming. 'Goodbye, Luca,' she said, as she turned away, her voice aching with an unspoken and totally inappropriate hunger.

Luca caught a whiff of her scent as her movement swirled and parted the air between them. He moved closer for a second infusion, placing his hand back up high on the doorframe. 'You don't wear your ring any more,' he said to her back. He had noticed it in the bush and it had bugged him ever since.

'No.' Her voice trembled and she swallowed.

Luca inched closer, his control hanging by a thread. 'We're still married,' he said huskily. 'Why did you take off?'

Rilla didn't turn round. Luca's presence loomed from behind, so very close, and she knew if she looked at him she'd be lost. 'It was time.'

She turned the knob but his hand prevented the door from opening. Blocking her freedom.

'Let me out.' Her voice sounded cracked and thready and she hated the naked streak of arousal so blatantly evident. There was an unbearable heat down low and her nipples were painfully tight.

Luca's heart drummed frantically as her smell worked its way past his diminishing resistance. It was Rilla's essence and he wanted to bite into her neck, slip his arms around her waist and re-acquaint himself with every inch of it.

Rilla couldn't stand the tension any longer. 'Please, Luca,' she half groaned, half whispered, her lips and body pressed against the wood of the door trying to escape the flare of his body heat behind her.

Luca was drawn like a moth to flame as he moved closer, pushing against the length of her. 'That's what you used to say,' he whispered, his lips in her hair. 'I missed it, Rilla.'

His breath caressed her scalp and her knees almost buckled at the husky timbre of his voice. His slight accent ruffled her name and a surge of pure want coursed through her. Rilla searched frantically through a brain that was powering down, seduced into standby mode by the feel of him, hard against her. Blood was being shunted to other areas of her body, tightening her breasts and pooling in her belly. She suddenly felt very, very awake.

This was madness. How could her body betray her so badly? She didn't want to want this.

'You're so beautiful,' Luca muttered, the hand he had up high on the doorjamb lowering to push her hair off her shoulder, exposing her neck. His fingers stroked the soft skin there and he gave a triumphant smile as she stretched it for better access. His hand tightened on her hip.

'Rilla?'

She swallowed. 'Luca, this is crazy.'

Yes, it was. But her voice was a hoarse plea that grated erotically along his nerve endings. His abdominal muscles contracted as if she'd trailed her nails across them. Luca put his hands on her shoulders and turned her round again. 'I know.'

She sank against the door, his aroused body pressed against the length of hers intimately. His breath was ragged, clearly audible, rubbing against her skin like sandpaper. She shouldn't want this. But she did. Seven years without his touch, seven years of absence disappeared in the fog of desire that encroached on her senses. It was as if nothing had ever come between them.

Luca wanted to kiss her more than he'd ever wanted anything. He lifted his hands to the cleavage of her shirt, to the top button straining to keep itself inside its hole. He looked at her, giving her a chance to pull back. Her tawny gaze glowed her surrender and he slowly popped each button in turn, exposing her chest to his hungry gaze.

Rilla moaned as the air hit her heated skin. The look of naked desire in his black, black eyes forced her to swallow hard. He was looking at her like he could devour her. His breathing was harsh as his gaze roamed over her greedily. She felt her nipples bead beneath the lacy fabric of her red bra and she almost arched her back in blatant invitation. Luca groaned, his gaze roaming over every luscious inch.

No one had ever looked at her like he did. No one. With eyes that stamped *Mine* all over her. She found it hard just to breathe under the weight of his possessive, hungry gaze. She should have felt objectified. But she didn't.

'I've dreamt about touching you. Like this,' he whispered, a finger following the swell of a breast down into her cleavage. The finger tracked the lace edge back out again and in one deft movement pushed the lacy cup aside and stroked an engorged dusky tip.

Rilla fought against the moan that rose in her throat. But it still found its way out. Part of her hated it that he could do this to her. Hated it that he could freeze her out for seven years and still her body flowered beneath his touch. Yearned for his touch.

Luca swooped his head the short distance to claim her mouth. The first touch of her lips was like throwing petrol on a fire and he pushed her hard against the door as he savaged her mouth. She moaned and he increased the pressure until he was plundering her sweetness so thoroughly he wasn't sure where she ended and he began.

God, he had missed this. Missed her. Despite everything, he wanted her as much as he ever had. 'Tell me you missed me,' he whispered against her mouth, his breathing coarse. He needed to hear he wasn't alone in this madness.

'I missed you,' she cried, no thought of denial as he created havoc of such delicious proportions she thought it might just kill her.

Luca wished that made it better. It didn't. This whole thing was making him crazy. Everything burned. His loins were on fire, his chest was bursting with the pounding of his heart, his brain exulted in their inevitable joining and railed against it too. Damn! He didn't want to want her this much. He was supposed to be seeking closure—not revisiting old ground.

'Yes,' she cried as his hand jerked aside the other bra cup and his lips closed over the turgid peak.

Rilla looked down at his dark head fastened at her breast and had such a fierce sense of possession it sucked her breath away. She plunged a hand into his hair, pressing him closer, arching her back, urging him to take more.

Everywhere ached, everywhere yearned. The tingling between her legs was almost unbearable and she reached for Luca's fly, impatient to feel him inside her. She moaned as her hand found his hot, naked length. The stray thought that he wasn't wearing any underwear floated out of reach as she squeezed him tight and Luca groaned into her neck.

He was as thick as she remembered, filling her palm and she slid her hand up and down the length of him a few times, refamilarising herself with his proportions.

His hands were hot on her skin as he pushed her skirt up. 'Hurry,' she panted as she guided his hardness towards her heat.

Luca lifted her up, his hands cupping her buttocks, fitting her against him as her tongue stroked against his, betraying her impatience for a much more intimate invasion. Her legs clamped around his waist and he pushed her hard against the door for better leverage.

He entered her in one decisive stroke, swallowing her cry with his mouth as he seared her lips with his. He groaned as she enveloped him in a tight velvet glove, the sensation too exquisite for him to even breathe.

He opened his eyes and eased himself away from her slightly, looking down at her. Her head was thrown back, her teeth biting her lower lip. Her breasts, partially released from their lacy prisons, were swollen and moist from his ministrations and he wanted more.

Rilla opened her eyes and regarded him through heavy lids. It felt good to be stretched all the way. She'd forgotten how well he filled her. 'Please,' she begged, 'don't stop.'

Luca groaned, thrilled at the sheer wantonness of her exposed flesh and the depth of her supplication. He sheathed himself again in her tight, moist depth.

'Luca,' she cried, fixing him with her amber

gaze as she clutched his shoulders, his entry rocking her head back against the door. His black eyes glittered back at her, like diamonds in coal.

'Again!' Rilla gasped, her gaze twisting with his as he obeyed her command. She pulled his head down and claimed his mouth in a kiss full of passion and seven years of denial.

She cried out as he slid into her. Once. Twice. Three times. She could feel her internal muscles start to tense and tighten around him. He groaned and she knew he could feel it too.

He lifted his head. Their gazes locked as their bodies moved to a rhythm that was innately them. Higher and higher. Closer and closer. Rilla fought against the rise. It swelled up and she beat it back, wanting to cherish this moment. Wanting it to last.

Luca groaned, his resolve to outlast her fraying by the second. The pressure in his loins built unbearably.

He lowered his head to her breasts and sucked each nipple deep into his mouth. He grunted at her strangled gasp and looked up into her face. She was walking the fine line between pleasure and pain and he wanted to, needed to, feel her come apart in his arms.

He buried his face in her neck, his forehead against the door. He turned so his lips were at her ear and he whispered words of lust and longing in his native tongue.

Rilla shivered as his breath caressed her ear and clutched his shoulders as the words destroyed her concentration. 'No…fair…Luca,' she cried as the words filled her head and flowed over her body like fine silk and warm honey.

'Come on, Rilla, come with me,' Luca whispered as he felt her muscles grip him hard and knew she was about to go over the edge. And he was right there with her.

'I hate it that you can still do this to me,' she sobbed as her orgasm rushed forward, unable to be held back after so much denial. She bucked against the door, her back arching.

He hated her power over him too. But then his own release joined hers and he couldn't think any more. He held her tight as for one elusive moment the world stopped and pleasure erupted around him, rained down on him. Then he rode it, rocking her against the door, stoking her release and his until there was nothing left, until they were breathless and spent.

The house was silent except for the sound of their uneven breathing. He stirred, raining gentle kisses over her face, whispering endearments in Italian, still locked inside her. 'Are you OK, *cara*?' he whispered.

Rilla could barely speak, never mind wrap her head around the explosion of passion she'd been at the centre of. 'I...don't know.'

'Shh,' Luca soothed, adjusting them so he could swing her into his arms. 'You're tired—we both are.' He carried her into his room and lowered her gently onto the bed, lying beside her, pulling her against him spoon fashion.

'Go to sleep,' he murmured into her hair, his own eyes unbearably heavy, post-coital fatigue melding with days of inadequate sleep.

Rilla knew she should be protesting the intimacy. Having sex against the front door was one thing. But spending the night in his bed, like lovers, like husband and wife, was another. But the intense orgasm had sapped what little reserves she had and she could feel the lure of sleep pulling her under even before her head hit the pillow.

She was out cold in seconds.

CHAPTER FOUR

THE sun, already high in the sky, finally penetrated Rilla's closed lids. She opened them slowly, taking a moment or two to orientate herself, last night returning in full Technicolor detail. She was alone and she didn't know whether to feel relieved or annoyed.

She looked down at her fully clothed form. Well, sort of fully clothed. Her red shirt was still undone and gaping open, revealing her bra. She blushed, thinking about how it had gotten that way, and wondered what Luca had thought when he'd woken this morning to see her goods on full display.

Had he tried to wake her? Her slumber had been so deep she doubted whether she'd even moved overnight. A nuclear explosion probably wouldn't have woken her this morning. Three days and nights of little sleep, the stress of Bridie's illness and a bone-melting orgasm had certainly taken their toll.

Rilla stretched and felt the ache of internal muscles that hadn't been used in a long time. Her teeth worried her bottom lip as she thought about their next meeting. Would it be awkward? Would they know what to say to each other? What were his expectations? Hell—what were hers?

She didn't know. She didn't know what it meant or how it would affect them working together or their looming divorce. She did know that last night hadn't been the wisest thing she'd ever done. In fact, muddying the waters that way had been incredibly stupid. And if she could undo it, she would.

Really.

Rilla turned her head to check the time. The red numbers told her it was eleven o'clock.

Eleven o'clock!

She vaulted into an upright position. She'd had no idea it was so late. Why had Luca let her sleep so long? Where was he? The house was as silent as a cemetery. Damn it! She should be at the hospital. He should have woken her. She needed a shower and a change of clothes and her car was still at the hospital. Argh!

An hour later, Rilla strode into the parents' lounge to find Gabe and Beth eating lunch.

'Afternoon, sleepyhead,' Beth teased.

Rilla felt the tension ooze out of her. Beth was looking rested and was showing some sass—Bridie must have had a good night. 'I take it everything's still going well?'

'By leaps and bounds,' Beth confirmed. 'Luca's in with her so we could eat together.'

Her heart gave a loud thud at the mention of Luca's name. So he was there? 'Oh,' Rilla said, trying for nonchalance. 'Has he been here long?'

'Couple of hours.' Gabe shrugged.

'Why don't you go and keep him company? We'll be another fifteen minutes or so,' Beth suggested.

Rilla's pulse reverberated through her entire body, her heart banging against her ribs as if it was trying to escape her chest as she approached Bridie's room. She was more nervous seeing him now than she had been the other morning at work with an audience of colleagues.

She drew level with the doorway to the isolation room and stopped short. Luca was stroking Bridie's head and murmuring to her in his native tongue, calling her his little bush *bambina*. He was looking at her with such compassion it sucked Rilla's breath away.

Was he thinking about their baby as he stroked Bridie's downy wisps? *As she was?* Wondering how different it could have been had she managed to carry their baby to full term. *As she was?* Fantasising about dribbly smiles, early-morning cuddles and soft baby skin? *As she was?*

Why had they let things go so cold between them?

Bridie's nurse spotted her in the doorway and told her to come in. Luca raised his head and she held her breath, unsure of what she would see in his eyes.

'Hello, Rilla.'

Rilla saw the same wariness she knew was reflected in her gaze. Did he regret their impulsiveness too? 'You should have woken me, Luca,' Rilla chided, as she walked to the other side of her niece's cot.

He was looking devastatingly casual in a polo shirt and jeans, and she wondered if they were the ones he'd been wearing last night. The ones she'd helped him out of.

Luca watched her approach, trying to gauge her state of mind. He noticed she'd showered and changed her clothes. Her hair was still wet and pulled back into a sleek ponytail. A sudden memory of him brushing her newly washed hair for her on their honeymoon reared up at him and he looked down at Bridie, unprepared for the mix of emotions it evoked.

'You were exhausted,' he dismissed.

She hadn't been too exhausted to cross a line that had been decisively drawn seven years ago.

Rilla also averted her gaze to her niece. Bridie was awake and looking around, her breathing tube and the brown tape holding it secure marring her cherubic features. Her tiny fingers grasped Luca's forefinger and Rilla was pleased for the distraction.

'Hello, sweetie,' Rilla crooned at her niece, because it was easier to talk to her than to face Luca.

After a few minutes of babbling to Bridie, aware of their pregnant silence, Rilla said, 'Beth was saying she had a good night.'

'Yes. They're talking about extubating her tomorrow.'

They made awkward small talk for the next ten minutes, talking to the nurse and to Bridie to avoid having to talk to each other.

'We're back,' Beth announced, entering the room holding Gabe's hand.

Rilla envied her sister's relationship. Gabe and Beth hadn't been together that long either, but Bridie's crisis had only strengthened their union. They were leaning on each other. Unlike them. First sign of a problem in their marriage and they'd fallen apart.

'Why don't you guys go and have lunch at the cafeteria?' Beth suggested. 'It's a beautiful day and I bet you raced to the hospital without eating anything, Rilla.'

It was true—she'd showered, changed and

then bolted over. And she was starving. She chanced a glance at Luca. He shrugged and raised an eyebrow at her and she nodded. There were things that had to be said. Next week they'd be working together again and they couldn't work as an effective team, crucial to emergency medicine, with last night dangling between them.

Luca waited until they were seated at one of the shaded outside tables before he launched straight into the speech he'd been practising.

'I'm sorry...about last night... It shouldn't have happened,' Luca said. 'I take full responsibility. I should have shown more restraint.' It was then he realised that he hadn't even thought about contraception. *Hell.*

'Don't,' Rilla said, holding up her hand and refusing to let him shoulder the blame. It was typical of Luca to want to protect her, but she was just as accountable. 'I wanted it as much as you did.'

'No.' He shook his head vigorously. 'You were tired. Your niece was ill. It was a...mistake.'

Rilla felt strangely miffed by his critical summation of their spontaneous passion. She knew he was right, that their relationship didn't need the complication, but as far as mistakes went, Rilla had made a few in her life and none of them had ever made her feel quite that good.

She shrugged, trying to be nonchalant. Like she had head-banging sex against doors with men every day of the week. 'People have sex with their exes all the time, Luca. I think it was probably inevitable. Now it's out of our systems, we can get on with our lives. We've banished the lust demons, so to speak. Cleared the air.'

'That was clearing the air?' he asked incredulously. Seven years of denial had culminated in a hell of a climax and banished nothing. In fact, his libido, non-existent for years, had suddenly roared to life.

How were they supposed to put their past behind them, work together after that? Maybe he should have thought his impulse to apply for the position at the General through a little better. Maybe he should have ignored the urge and stayed in the UK. But the divorce papers arriving out of the blue after seven years of silence had thrown him, and he hadn't questioned the whim to return.

Rilla blushed. OK, maybe that was simplifying it too much, considering her entire body still throbbed with his possession. Sitting opposite him now, his masculinity a potent aphrodisiac, she realised it had just whetted her appetite. Exacerbated the desire she'd kept a tight lid on for the last seven years.

'I just think we should put last night in context. You said you came back for closure. I think we both got that last night. One last hurrah, so to speak. The important thing is we have to work together, Luca. I've worked hard to establish my career. I'm up for the NUM position and I can't let anything derail my focus. Sign the papers, Luca. Let's put an end to it so we can both move forward.'

Rilla paused, proud of her rock-solid delivery. Inside she was quaking but she knew it had sounded succinct and confident. They could analyse last night until the cows came home. It was what they did from now on that mattered.

'You've changed,' Luca murmured. She was decisive. Taking the lead. Confident. Not the Rilla who had been happy just being part of them.

Rilla shrugged. 'I grew up, Luca. I had a miscarriage. We grew apart. You left.'

Luca winced at her ruthless but concise summation of their downward spiral.

'Did you expect to come back and find me pining for you?'

Had he? Luca didn't know. He would have been sorely disappointed if he had. She hadn't even kept her wedding ring on. 'I don't know, Rilla.'

Rilla searched his face for a sign of his real motives. For something to make sense of his reappearance. She found nothing in his schooled features. His black eyes were unreadable, his face carefully neutral. So different from last night.

She'd seen that look too many times before. Even when she had told him to leave he had looked at her with that frustrating distance in his gaze. 'Did you even think about me, Luca?' she asked.

Every day. I picked up the phone to ring you

every day for two years. 'More than was good for my sanity.'

Rilla felt her heart stop in her chest before resuming at an erratic pace. She hadn't expected to hear the wrenched admission.

'And you?' he asked.

'You were my husband. I loved you. You were never far from my thoughts.'

Luca felt the husky timbre of her voice right down to his groin. 'Am. Present tense. I am your husband.'

Rilla looked at him incredulously. Just because they'd had sex, it didn't make them a couple again again. Too much time had passed. If it had only been two years or even five, she could have still held out hope. But his distance and his silence had gradually killed anything she'd ever felt for him.

'No. Luca. You are my estranged husband. One signature and you're my ex-husband. Let's not kid ourselves that last night was any more than a unique situation fuelled by emotion and fatigue.'

'And you think we can work together again with last night between us?'

They had to. She'd worked too long and too hard to jeopardise her chances at the top job now. 'We're not teenagers, Luca,' she said, not bothering to disguise her annoyance. 'With any luck I'm about to land the NUM position. Whether we like it or not, we're going to have to get along. Do I think we can ever go back to the way we used to work together? No. But, then, we're no longer lowly registrar and junior nurse. You're the consultant and I'm pretty sure I'm going to be NUM. People will be looking to us to lead. I know we can treat each other with respect and collegial propriety. In fact, I expect it. Will that be a problem for you?'

Yes and no. Certainly he would show her the same respect he'd always shown her at work as an important and integral part of the team. Someone whose opinion he valued highly. But even now, sitting opposite her, despite her assertions they'd exorcised their lust demons, he knew he wanted her again. Would that get worse, seeing her every day?

'No problem,' Luca assured her.

Rilla expelled the breath she'd been holding

when it had looked like he was about to argue. 'Good.' She swallowed the remnants of her coffee. 'In that case I look forward to working with you again, Dr Romano.'

She offered her hand and was pleased when he encompassed it in a firm grip.

'And you, Sister Winters.'

She ignored the mad flutter of the pulse at her wrist as his low voice stroked her skin and his hand lingered. She extracted hers determinedly. There was no space in her life to indulge in fluttering pulses.

Rilla returned to work on Monday, knowing that Bridie was out of PICU and probably going to be discharged from the kids' ward tomorrow. The fact that Hailey worked there and would be looking out for their niece doubled Rilla's confidence.

All she had to worry about now was the fact that it was Luca's first day at the hospital. A ball of nervous energy sat in the pit of her stomach as she worried how their first day back at work together would pan out. She'd only caught the odd glance of him over the last few days as he'd popped in to see Bridie each day, and knowing that she would be seeing him every day was daunting to say the least.

She was also acutely aware that too much of the space in her head in the last few days had been taken up by their explosive joining. It had replayed over and over in her mind. She'd looked at it from every angle, analysed it, berated herself over it and dreamt about it at night in surround-sound, giant-plasma-screen detail.

And she still wasn't sure what to make of it.

But she was sure of one thing. Their unexpected intimacy complicated her determination to keep their relationship strictly professional.

The first person she saw as she walked through the door for her late shift was Luca. He was sitting at the central desk and their gazes locked. There was a brief flare in his eyes, a reaction that she recognised as purely physical, before he blinked and his gaze became warily neutral.

'Rilla.' He nodded his head. 'How are you?'

'Good, thank you,' she said, fixing a smile on her face as she calmly walked by.

* * *

A few hours later a young man walked through the sliding doors as Rilla swept past on her way to greet an arriving ambulance.

'Are you OK?' she asked, gesturing to the young man to take a seat.

Both hands were grasping his neck, one on either side just below his ears. His fingers were splayed wide, his thumbs stretching to meet beneath his chin. He was holding his head very still and a frown knitted his brows together.

'It'll probably sound really silly,' he said.

Rilla ruefully wished she had a dollar for every time she'd heard that in the emergency department. But the young man was abnormally still, barely even opening his mouth widely enough to be understood, and she could see a hint of fear in his gaze. She smiled encouragingly. 'Did you do something to your neck?'

'I don't recall doing anything but...' He paused. 'This sounds so dumb...my head feels like it's going to fall off.'

Rilla smiled again while every cell in her body grew instantly alarmed. 'OK, right. Well, first things first. We're going to get a collar on you and get a doctor to see you.'

Immediately.

She smiled at him again. 'What's your name?' she asked as she gestured to Emily, the ward clerk at the triage desk.

'Damien.'

'Hi, Damien. I'm Rilla.'

Emily approached. 'Ems, can you find a nurse and tell them I need a cervical collar, please?'

Rilla hoped she sounded calm and professional because somewhere deep in her gut she knew that Damien had probably fractured his neck and was a walking time bomb.

She turned back to her patient. 'We'll get you into a cubicle. You're going to need some X-rays.'

Damien started to haul himself out of the chair. 'Just tell me where.'

Rilla placed an urgent stilling hand on Damien's arm as her pulse leapt. 'Collar first.' She smiled calmly.

A junior nurse appeared with a cervical collar and Rilla utilised her to keep Damien's neck motionless while she applied it. She held her breath until it was firmly in place.

'Hell. That's really uncomfortable.'

Rilla smiled. 'Good, it's on properly, then.' She placed an arm underneath his elbow, indicating for him to come with her.

'There's something wrong with my neck, isn't there?' Damien asked, resisting her pull.

Rilla looked down into his anxious gaze. She doubted he was even twenty. But his eyes looked intelligent and she knew he didn't want to be placated. 'Yes. I think so.'

She saw the panic take hold then and placed her hand over his. 'Let's get the tests done and get you seen by the right people first. We have the very best,' she assured him, smiling with an air of absolute confidence. 'OK?'

She saw some of the dread recede. One thing Rilla knew for sure, here at the Brisbane General, Damien's injury couldn't be in better hands.

Rilla was helping Damien onto a bed when Luca entered the cubicle.

'What have we got?' he asked.

Rilla took a deep breath at the sudden jolt through her solar plexus. She hadn't been prepared for him. Which was stupid. She'd known that consulting with Luca was bound to happen sooner or later. May as well get it out of the way early.

She listed Damien's symptoms and her treatment to date, proud of her professional detachment. Luca nodded at each salient point but didn't look at her and she was pleased to be spared the intensity of his black-velvet gaze.

'What have you been doing to yourself?' Luca asked. His tone was deliberately light, hiding the alarm at what he felt was almost certainly a potentially catastrophic injury. He glanced at Rilla, seeing her teeth sink betrayingly into her bottom lip, the way they always had when she was deeply concerned. She knew it too.

'Just woke up with a bit of a sore neck this morning and it's been getting worse all day.' Damien shrugged. Or as much as he could with a collar that was applied so tightly it restricted shoulder movement as well.

'What about last night?' Luca probed. 'Yesterday?'

'Just some footy with my mates at a back-yard barbie last night. It was a bit of a late one. Didn't get home till after four.'

'Footy? Did you fall? Get tackled?' Luca cut straight to the salient point.

Damien frowned. 'Of course I did. No more than usual, though. You don't feel anything after a few beers.'

Rilla felt sick. Had Damien been walking around with a fractured neck since last night? She glanced at Luca and could tell by the way his jaw clenched and unclenched that he was also very worried.

'So you have pain in your neck?' Luca asked.

'Oh yeah.'

'Any numbness, or tingling in your arms or legs?' Luca persisted.

'Nope,' Damien replied.

'Any difficulties swallowing, coughing or breathing?'

'None,' Damien said.

'OK. Right.' Luca nodded, relieved to see that

there were no gross cord compression symptoms. 'I'm sending you for an MRI.' He took his stethoscope from around his neck. 'Rilla, can you page the neurology team?'

Luca knew the moment she'd left and he felt the tension across his shoulders ease. He'd been acutely aware of her presence— even her lingering perfume interfered with his concentration.

'Right, let's get a full neuro assessment.'

'Now you're scaring me, Doc.'

Luca pulled up a stool, fairly certain that Damien's life was about to change significantly. 'I think you may have damaged your neck. I'm not sure of the severity yet. It may be nothing.'

Rilla watched Luca talking to their patient from the central work station through the partially open curtain as she waited for the neuro team to get back to her. She couldn't hear what he was saying but she could hear the low rumble of his voice and noticed how he had placed a hand on Damien's shoulder.

She watched as the frown between Damien's eyes smoothed out and he actually smiled for the first time since walking through the doors. Luca's bedside manner had always been second to none. She'd seen his quiet confidence, innate Latin charm and easy smile calm everyone from the most fractious child to the most frightened heart-attack patient. It had been one of the things that had attracted her most.

He'd always been a pleasure to watch in action and not even their complicated history could erase the fact. The phone rang and she answered it, relaying the details of Damien's case to the neuro registrar.

Rilla re-entered the cubicle, efficiently flicking the curtain shut. 'They'll be here shortly,' she said briskly.

'Excellent,' Luca said. He patted Damien's shoulder. 'Rilla will get your details and I'll be back when the neurologist arrives.'

He turned to leave. 'Well caught,' he said in a low voice as he passed her on his way out.

Rilla turned back to Damien, smiling to herself. She couldn't help it. Even after seven years, his praise still made her glow.

* * *

Just before her evening meal break Rilla was relieving an exhausted mother of her wheezy eighteen-month-old daughter so she could administer a ventolin nebuliser. The restless infant smelled like soap and sunshine and Rilla's heart contracted as the little girl snuffled tiredly into her neck, the toddler's hair brushing against her face.

She hugged the little one close. An overwhelming urge to have a baby of her own washed over her and she absently kissed the toddler's head. *How many babies would she and Luca have had by now?*

As if by some extrasensory connection, Luca chose that moment to enter the cubicle and their gazes locked over the child's head. Was he thinking the same thing? He looked tall and lean and sexy as hell, and her pulse leapt.

'I thought you left at five.' She blurted the first thing that came into her head in an effort to banish oestrogen-enriched fantasies.

Luca's breath caught in his throat at the sight of Rilla rocking the fretful child, trying to balance it and hold the misting mask in place as she clucked soothingly.

'I was just on my way out. The regs looked snowed under.'

Rilla nodded. It had been crazy for the last two hours.

Luca turned to the mother. 'How's she doing?' He smiled, consulting the chart at the end of the trolley.

'Better, I think. But still wheezy.'

Luca nodded as he placed his stethoscope in his ears and turned his attention to the child. The toddler had a chubby hand on Rilla's breast, squishing into the buxom roundness beneath Rilla's shirt, and its cheek against the hollow of her shoulder. She looked so maternal that Luca gripped the stethoscope hard, sucked into a past that never was.

'Hey, there, sweetie,' Luca crooned, and rubbed the little one's back.

The child turned her head towards his voice and Luca smiled at her. 'It's OK, it won't take long,' he said softly as he lifted her top so he could place the stethoscope against her chest.

The little girl settled a little, seemingly fascinated by Luca, and Rilla wasn't surprised. She was finding him pretty fascinating herself. It was hard to believe that after seven years' absence she could look her fill whenever she wanted. Even though it was a rather dangerous indulgence, considering their most recent episode.

She watched him as he fixed his gaze on the child's back and concentrated on the lung sounds. She waited for him to finish and swapped the child to her other hip so he could listen to the front.

'The wheezing is settling,' Luca said, addressing the anxious mother. 'We'll see how it is after a few more nebs.'

The mother smiled her gratitude as her daughter drifted off to sleep in Rilla's arms and then excused herself, using the moment to escape for a much-needed loo break.

Luca and Rilla were left alone in the cubicle, a drowsy child and all the missed opportunities it represented between them. Rilla rubbed her chin absently along the child's head, excruciatingly aware of the intimate undercurrent.

Luca's gaze followed the sweep of her hair tied back in a ponytail, the soft skin of her neck temptingly vulnerable. At another time he might have drawn her close and pressed his lips to it. But that time was long gone.

He roused himself from the clutches of the past, clearing his throat. 'I actually came to tell you that Damien's MRI showed he has a fractured C1. It's stable but he's going to Theatre to have a Halo fitted. He'll spend a couple of days on the spinal unit then he should be able to be managed as an outpatient until it's healed.'

Rilla blinked, dragging herself out of the mire of past emotions. It was good news for Damien and she was pleased to know he'd presented in time. Walking around with an undiagnosed neck fracture had disaster written all over it.

'Thank you for letting me know,' she said quietly.

Luca nodded. 'No problem.'

Rilla continued to rock the toddler as the neb mask spluttered the last of the medication, hyper-aware of Luca standing watching her.

'OK, then. I guess I'll see you tomorrow,' Luca said, edging towards the curtain. He flicked it open and halted, turning back to face her. 'It's been great working with you today. I've missed it.'

Rilla looked at him, startled by his admission. It *had* been just like old times but this little tête-à-tête was far from collegial. There was a most definite undercurrent. And that just wouldn't do. 'Go home, Luca. You've been here for twelve hours.'

Her low voice swirled around him and he stared at the flare of heat in her amber gaze for a long moment. She was right. He'd been there way too long. 'Goodnight.'

Rilla watched the empty space where he'd been for a long moment, annoyed at the loud thump of her heart.

Damn him for coming back.

CHAPTER FIVE

THE next month flew by. Rilla was up to her elbows in collating two lots of research she'd been involved with, staying back most nights and coming in on her days off, shut away in Julia's office, working on the computer. If she did get the NUM position, she wanted to be on top of everything.

Her nervousness grew as each day passed. Ever since the miscarriage and Luca pulling away from her, she'd thrown herself into work, dedicated her life to her career, and the NUM position had been firmly in her sights.

The odds were in her favour too. She'd acted in the position numerous times, covering for Julia's annual leave, and had been second-in-charge for five years. She knew the job, the staff and the hospital back to front. But that didn't mean that a better-qualified outside applicant couldn't still snatch it from her. She knew they'd interviewed six people for the position over a period of a month.

At least she had plenty to distract her from Luca. He was everywhere and even when she couldn't see him or hear his laughter filtering around the department, everyone was talking about him.

The new consultant was a huge hit. The registrars and residents loved him and the nurses weren't far behind. Every female with a pulse in the department, including the cleaner, drooled over his dark Latin looks and sexy accent. He smiled and joked with them all, teaching happily and effortlessly putting everyone at ease. Within a month he'd totally endeared himself.

Rilla kept their dealings strictly professional, as did Luca, but even so it took a supreme effort not to get sucked back into the Luca worship vortex. They'd had their chance and blown it. Nothing could be gained from walking that road again.

She still hadn't seen the divorce papers and knew she was going to have to raise the matter with him again. The simple truth of the matter was that she didn't need him to sign them to lodge them. It was symbolic more than anything. His acknowledgement that it was over. A statement that they both knew there was nothing left of them.

After the job, she told herself. As soon as she knew the outcome of the interview, she'd talk to Luca about it. But for now she wanted to concentrate all her good energy and positive vibes on being the successful applicant.

It was a Thursday afternoon in mid-October when she was called into Julia's office and given the good news. As of January, she would be the new nurse unit manager of the department of emergency medicine at the Brisbane General.

Rilla was ecstatic, hugging Julia repeatedly. Finally, after years of striving towards her goal, it was hers!

'Drinks at Barney's tonight,' she announced to all and sundry as they passed the central work station. 'First round on me.'

It felt good to join the regular work crowd at

Barney's for their afternoon drinks. She had forgone the ritual the last few weeks, preferring not to push the boundaries of collegiality with Luca. But today there was much to celebrate. And Rilla couldn't think of a better way than a couple of hours of shooting the breeze with her colleagues.

Less than an hour later, however, she was feeling quite differently. She'd been perfectly fine and then suddenly she was sitting there, her face aching with the effort of keeping her smile in place while nausea sat like a lead sinker in the pit of her stomach.

She'd had a funny tummy the last few days. Nothing too dire, just a vague queasiness. And she'd been incredibly tired, even in the mornings. But she'd been working like a dog, pushing herself with the research. Maybe she'd just overdone things and become run down?

Her second orange juice sat untouched before her as the fake citrus aroma assaulted her. She was acutely aware of the heavy mix of colognes surrounding her, of the cigarette smoke coming from the slot-machine area, of beer and cooking steaks.

It had been like that at work too, she belatedly realised. She'd found herself hyper-sensitive to the usual mix of aromas that as a nurse she'd previously been immune to—disinfectant, IV antibiotics, concentrated urine, vomit and infected wounds.

A waitress walked past with some cappuccinos and the strong aroma of coffee had her on her feet in an instant.

'Excuse me,' she said, hoping she didn't look as desperate as she felt, quickly making her way to the toilets. She made it just in time, retching and retching until her stomach ached and her head spun.

It took ten minutes for the nausea to subside and the shaking to stop and for her legs to feel they could support her. She rose from the tiled floor, splashed water on her face at the basins and then wearily made her way back to the table. She gathered her bag and made her excuses amidst a chorus of protests and left.

The fresh air felt marvellous on her heated skin as she left Barney's. Several people pushed past her on their way in and Rilla stumbled and would have fallen had a warm hand under her elbow not prevented it.

'Oh, thank you,' she said, closing her eyes as a wave of dizziness followed hot on the heels of a fresh bout of nausea.

She opened them again to find eyes as black as a starless night looking back at her.

'Rilla?' Luca's gaze raked over her. He knew every nuance of every facial expression she possessed. She looked pale and shaken. She was obviously unwell. 'Are you OK?' he demanded.

His words were drowned out by the roar of a truck as it thundered past, spewing diesel fumes. The acrid aroma misted Rilla in its cloying cloud and she mewed as she looked around desperately for somewhere to be sick and not disgrace herself in front of the busy evening trade.

An alley ran down beside Barney's and she wrenched away from Luca, stumbling into the dark recess. She bent over, splaying her legs wide, and retched again, hoping to God that Luca hadn't followed. Nothing came up.

'What's wrong?'

His Italian shoes appeared in her line of vision

and even through her misery she could hear the concern in his voice. She wanted to lean her head against the brick wall and cry.

Rilla felt the nausea subside and righted herself slowly, her hand against the rough brick. She turned and leaned heavily against the wall as her pulse hammered madly through her head.

'Are you…? Have you drunk too much?'

Had she the energy Rilla would have laughed in his face. She was suddenly bone tired. 'Don't be so ridiculous,' she said wearily. 'I have to drive.'

Muted neon bled into the soft blanket of twilight and stabbed into the narrow passage, throwing his face into shadow. He looked dark and dangerous. Not someone anyone would want to be stuck with in a rapidly darkening alley.

'Are you ill?' he demanded.

Rilla pushed away from the wall and started back down the alley. She felt wretched and all she wanted was her bed. 'I think I'm coming down with a virus,' she muttered.

'Have you seen someone about it?' he asked, calling after her.

Rilla ignored him, concentrating on putting one foot in front of the other. If he wanted to talk to her, he could keep up.

'I said,' Luca said, catching up to her and snagging her arm, pulling her around and back into the privacy of the alley, 'have you seen someone about it?'

'Luca, I'm really tired and—'

The persistent nausea ratcheted up another notch and she put her hand out to lean against the brick wall.

Luca saw her sway and realised she was barely keeping upright. *'Dio!'* he swore, and swept her up in his arms and strode out of the alley, ignoring her protests. The green man was flashing at the pedestrian crossing and he carried her across the road.

'Put me down, Luca,' Rilla admonished as she clung around his neck. People in the street around them were staring and she felt heat rise in her cheeks.

'You're not well. I'm taking you home,' Luca said, holding her tighter as she squirmed.

'Are you going to carry me all the way?' Rilla

asked, not really objecting terribly much any more. She relaxed into him, snuggling her head against his shirt, just too weary to care.

'No, just to my car,' he said as he came up alongside it and pushed the button on his keys to open the central locking. 'I'm putting you down now. Will you be OK?' he asked.

Rilla was vaguely aware that he was talking to her and she murmured, 'Yes.'

Luca lowered her to the ground reluctantly. It had felt good to hold her in his arms again. She had felt warm and soft against him and her breath had been warm against his neck, her lips almost touching it.

He kept hold of her as he opened the passenger door and she swayed into him, her hip and breast rubbing against the fabric of his clothes. 'Hop in,' he said, a husky note threading through his voice.

Rilla roused herself as he gently guided her into the seat. 'But I have my own car,' she said, resisting.

'You are in no fit state to drive,' Luca said firmly as he coaxed her into his sporty BMW. 'It'll be safe in the General's car park overnight,' he said patiently as he knelt beside her and lifted her legs into the car. 'I'll drop you back in the morning.'

Rilla blinked as the car door closed and she inhaled the fragrance of leather as she settled into the soft bucket seat. She waited for the nausea and was relieved to discover it was gone. Luca climbed in beside her and didn't say a word as he buckled up and started the engine.

Rilla was asleep in less than thirty seconds. The low growl of the engine hummed like a lull-abye around her and she couldn't remember having felt this tired. She stirred slightly, her eyes heavy as she realised Luca didn't know her address, but then the thought slipped out of her grasp and disappeared into the blissful oblivion.

Luca drove calmly, despite the emotional squall lashing his insides. He was excruciatingly aware of her beside him. Even after all these years she still had a power over him that he'd thought he'd exorcised long ago. Of course, sleeping with her again hadn't helped in that regard.

Her head lolled towards the window and he swallowed as his gaze tracked the olive column of her neck. His fingers itched to stroke the skin there and he tightened them around the wheel. His eyes were drawn to her hands clasped low across her stomach, and he felt something stir inside. Their child had once grown there. He gripped the steering-wheel harder.

A thought occurred to him as he decelerated approaching a red light. Maybe it wasn't a virus? Maybe it was something else?

Tiredness and nausea. Two very common, classic symptoms of pregnancy.

He felt his pulse pound through his abdomen. Could it be? Luca tried to stay calm and rationalise. It probably was just a virus. She'd been keeping long hours the last month, longer than him, and prior to that there had been the stress of Bridie's illness. Maybe she'd left herself susceptible to an opportunistic infection.

But then he did a quick calculation—it had been a month since their night together in his bed.

And they hadn't used protection.

Luca didn't know what it was. Maybe it was the way she had her hands, as if she was cradling a fragile little life, or maybe it was the damn papers in his desk drawer that taunted him every day, but suddenly he had a very strong feeling, a gut feeling, that Rilla wasn't suffering from a virus.

If she was pregnant, did she know? Was she hiding it from him? Luca frowned. He didn't think so. She genuinely thought she was run down—he'd stake his life on it. He passed a late-night pharmacy and quickly pulled the car over. Rilla murmured but didn't wake, and he was in and out in two minutes.

'Rilla.' His voice was annoyingly husky in the hushed confines of the car and he cleared his throat. His brain had been formulating plans for the last few minutes and he was eager to get the ball rolling. 'Rilla,' he said again. Firmer. Louder.

'Hmm?' Rilla stirred.

Luca watched as her eyes fluttered open and the slumberous look tinted her amber eyes an amazing shade of gold. She looked vulnerable and he felt a fist claw at his gut.

Rilla almost sighed when she saw the soft black of Luca's eyes staring back at her. 'Are we here?' she asked.

Her sleepy voice and lazy smile were a potently sexy combination and Luca had to physically draw back from the temptation. 'At my place, yes,' he said, unbuckling his seat belt and getting out of the car before he did something truly insane like kiss her.

Rilla sat up and looked out the window. Luca's flat. Their flat. 'I thought you were taking me home?' she said as he opened the door and she allowed him to take her elbow and guide her out.

'My place was closer.' He shrugged. 'You're not well. I want to be able to keep an eye on you.'

'But—'

'Rilla!' Luca interrupted. 'Just humour me, OK?'

Rilla knew she shouldn't. She knew it was dangerous but would it hurt to let him take charge for one night? She was tired down to her bones and her stomach ached from being empty and ejecting its contents.

'You know you really need to work on your flattery, Luca,' she grumbled as she shut the car door and pushed away from the car.

'Hey,' Luca said, putting a hand on her elbow and drawing her back towards him so he could pick her up.

'Oh, no,' Rilla said, stepping out of his reach. 'I'm fine now. I can walk.'

'You're weak,' Luca insisted.

'I'm fine,' Rilla repeated, jutting her chin and staring him down.

Luca saw the determined look in her eyes and he acquiesced, but kept a guiding hand beneath her elbow. He unlocked the front door and pushed it shut behind them.

A vision of him taking her against it swamped him and he took a deep steadying breath before he turned back to her.

'We need to talk,' he said.

'Not now, Luca, please. I'm tired and desperately need a shower,' Rilla said.

'In a moment,' he said, steering her into the lounge and towards the couch.

'Luca,' she protested weakly.

'Sit,' he ordered, giving her a gentle push, knowing that she was so out on her feet a puff of wind could have blown her over.

He held out the brown packet in which the pharmacy had put his purchase. 'This is for you,' he said.

Rilla gave him an exasperated look as she took it. 'What is it?'

'Open it.'

Rilla rolled her eyes but opened the bag, not remotely curious. She could barely keep her eyes open. She pulled out a long rectangular box and looked at it for several moments through bleary eyes before it made any sense. It was a home pregnancy test kit.

'What the…?' she said, her tired brain not quite computing the meaning as she looked at him.

Luca knelt down. 'You're tired. You're nauseous. And it's been a month since we had sex. Unprotected sex. Are you still on the Pill?'

Rilla stared at the box in a daze. 'No. But…I

had my period,' she murmured, her brain coming awake now.

Luca's face fell. He felt stupidly disappointed. His planning on the drive hadn't involved the not-pregnant contingency. His gut feelings had always been spot on.

'It was pretty light, though. Didn't last long,' Rilla admitted. 'I just put it down to all the stress with Bridie and work.'

She was fully awake now. 'Do you think…?' She looked into Luca's deep black gaze. 'Do you think I could be pregnant?' She didn't even dare hope.

'I think it's a possibility. I think we should find out.'

Rilla looked at the box. The one thing she wanted more than anything else. More than Luca to sign the papers. More than the NUM position. Could it be true?

'Is your bladder full? Why don't you go and use it?' Luca suggested. The suspense was killing him but he could see Rilla was still processing the idea. He waited for a few more moments to prompt her. 'Rilla?'

'Hmm?' she said, looking at him. His gaze was carefully neutral but there was a betraying nerve jumping under his left eye and she could tell he was clenching his jaw. The outcome would affect him as much as her. 'Oh, yes, right.'

She rose, clutching the box for dear life.

'I'll be right out here,' Luca said as Rilla shut the toilet door on him.

Rilla's heart pounded and her hand shook as she opened the box. Could she really be pregnant? She pulled the toilet lid down and sat on it for a moment, absorbing the idea. Her hand found her abdomen and she placed it there, hoping for some psychic impulse to overcome her.

Luca paced for five minutes. What was taking her so long? The test only took two minutes, for crying out loud. He knocked lightly on the door. 'Rilla? Everything all right?'

Rilla came out of her daze. 'Er…yes, everything's good.'

'Have you done it?' He tried not to be impatient but he felt excluded from the first indication of his baby and he needed to know.

'Sorry… Hang on, doing it now.' Rilla took a deep breath, almost too frightened to carry it out. What if it was negative?

She rose and performed the necessary procedure but when it came to looking at the little window, she just couldn't. It was like her whole future depended on one little cross and she couldn't bear to look.

She opened the door and thrust the test at Luca. 'Here, you watch it,' she said, brushing past him to wash her hands in the bathroom.

Luca's eyes were drawn to the plastic stick with the two windows. The test window had its pink line clearly visible to prove that the test was viable, and before his eyes a pink cross slowly appeared in the other window.

It took a few moments for the implication to sink in to Luca's consciousness. It gradually took hold as a reality and Luca felt a joy welling in him that he couldn't deny. It started at his toes and worked its way through his body like a series of fireworks on New Year's Eve. His heart beat with the pop and swirl of light and colour.

Could it really be true? After all their history,

all their misery, could something so wonderful actually have happened? He could barely move for fear the moment would disappear.

He wanted this baby. He wanted this baby more than he'd ever wanted anything.

It was impractical. Inconvenient. They were almost divorced. But he wanted it anyway.

Rilla came out of the bathroom to see Luca holding the test up, a wide grin breaking across his handsome face. His eyes were glittering like moonlight on water. A little pink plus sign stared back at her.

She was pregnant.

She stared at the test, wanting to believe it but too afraid to allow herself, quashing the excited flutter dancing through her heart. 'What if it's wrong?' she murmured.

'It's not,' Luca said, and grinned again. Modern urine test kits were widely used in all kinds of medical facilities as a reliable, quick, cheap method of confirming pregnancy.

He wanted to pick her up and twirl her around. The distance between them on such an intimate occasion seemed all wrong. But this was a big event and he didn't want to put one foot wrong. Especially when she still seemed so disbelieving.

Rilla shook her head as it slowly sank in. *She was pregnant.* The baby she'd coveted for the last few years was now a reality. She placed a hand on her belly. She was going to be a mother. Luca's child was snuggling into her womb and as the news finally permeated she allowed the joy full rein.

She felt light. Lighter than she'd ever been. And happy. Stupidly, crazily, insanely happy. Despite a hundred reasons to be the complete opposite.

She reached for the test and took it from him. 'I don't believe it.' She shook her head.

'Believe it,' Luca whispered.

She looked at him. 'I don't know what to say.'

Luca grinned at her dazed expression. 'We need to talk. Why don't you go and have that shower and I'll fix us something to eat?'

Rilla nodded, on autopilot again, her brain utterly preoccupied with the stunning news. The fact that all she'd wanted when she'd walked into the flat fifteen minutes ago had been a shower and bed was completely lost on her. But she went through the motions anyway. Undressing, getting under the spray, applying soap.

She turned off the taps a few minutes later and found a pair of Luca's cotton boxers and a T-shirt hanging next to a towel on the rail. Not even the thought that he'd been in the room while she'd showered was enough to shift her focus from the baby.

She cleared the condensation from the bathroom mirror and inspected her reflection, turning to one side, smoothing her hand against her stomach. Water droplets beaded her skin but all she had to show was the same slight rise that always greeted her in the mirror.

Soon, though, it would blossom with Luca's child and she couldn't wait to see it grow large and full. Or for her breasts to become lush and spill out of her bra as they prepared to nurture Luca's baby. She pushed out her stomach as far as it would go and grinned stupidly at the woman in the mirror.

Oh, how different she felt this time round.

She flattened her stomach as thoughts of her first pregnancy intruded. She remembered looking at the stick with its two pink lines and feeling a gamut of emotions. She'd been twenty-two and married for just one month.

And then there'd been the dreadful end just five weeks later. A miscarriage that had not only halted their parental dreams but had been the beginning of the end for their marriage.

Rilla clutched her stomach, feeling fear break through her joy. The thought of losing another baby, of losing this baby, was too heart-wrenching to bear. She couldn't go through that again. She just couldn't. She didn't know anything about what the next few years would hold or what this baby meant for their impending divorce. She just knew she wanted it more than life itself.

Suddenly depressed, she dressed in the clothes Luca had put out, tying a knot in the T-shirt at her waist. Then she rummaged around in the bathroom drawer and located a packaged toothbrush. There were tears in her eyes as she watched her reflection. *Please, let nothing happen to my baby.*

She found Luca in the kitchen, preparing some food as soft strains of music swirled through the air. She watched him from the doorway, enjoying how he moved. He'd taken his tie off and undone the top two buttons of his shirt, and her fingers, tricked into some renegade sense of déjà vu, itched to push through his hair and bend his head down for a kiss.

Thinking about the miscarriage had dampened her mood and she could feel her earlier debilitating tiredness returning. Suddenly she didn't know what to say to him. She needed time to absorb the situation. To think. To be alone.

'I think I'm going to hit the sack,' she said casually.

Luca looked up from his chopping. She was wearing the clothes he had put out for her. His shirt was too big, falling off one shoulder and exposing her smooth olive skin to his view, and the way she'd tied it emphasised her waist and pulled across her braless chest. It had never looked so good.

He swallowed. 'You need to eat something first.'

Rilla's stomach revolted and she placed a hand over it. She shook her head. 'I can't.'

Luca watched the movement and itched to walk over to her and place his hand over hers. Over their baby. 'You have to eat, Rilla.'

Rilla was growing wearier by the second. It had been a day of huge climaxes and she was coming down from the high, feeling oddly disconnected. 'I just feel a little too delicate at the moment. And I'm tired, Luca.'

'It's only eight. We need to talk.'

'I know,' she sighed.

'What are we going to do?'

Good question. *Very good question.* 'Tomorrow, OK?' She knew they had to sit down and discuss things but, early evening or not, she could barely keep her eyes open. 'I promise.'

Luca nodded reluctantly. He could see her weariness and he didn't want to push her in her condition, but there were things he needed to know. He needed a plan. She was having his baby. *His baby.* And he wasn't going to mess it up this time.

'The spare room's made up.'

Rilla locked gazes with Luca for a brief intense moment, sensing his struggle. 'Thank you.'

Less than a minute later her head hit the pillow and she slept instantly.

CHAPTER SIX

LUCA woke the next morning to the sound of Rilla retching. He sat bolt upright as he looked at the clock. Six a.m. He was out of bed and striding to the bathroom before any other coherent thought had formed.

She was kneeling on the cold tiles, her forehead on the toilet seat. 'Rilla!'

'Go away,' she groaned as another urge to vomit took hold and she dry-retched into the bowl.

Luca knelt beside her, feeling helpless, and rubbed the small of her back. He lifted a strand of hair that had fallen forward and tucked it behind her ear. He murmured soothing words in Italian to her as she continued to be sick.

Rilla heard them through her primal noises and even though she had no idea what they meant, the low rumble of his voice was so comforting she just wanted to crawl onto his lap and feel his arms around her.

God, she felt awful!

It was another few minutes before the nausea released her from its grip and she felt hot tears well in her eyes and track down her face as she sat back on her haunches. She couldn't have stemmed them had her life depended on it. Great. As if it wasn't bad enough that Luca had to witness her vomiting, now he was being treated to a fit of self-pity.

'Hush,' he crooned softly as he rose to wet a washcloth and then gently wipe her blotchy face.

Rilla felt the reviving effects of the cool cloth instantly and her sobs soon died to the odd hic-coughy breath. 'I'm sorry,' she whispered, almost falling into his soft velvet gaze.

'Hey, it's OK,' Luca whispered, and drew her head onto his shoulder while he continued to rub her back.

Rilla became conscious then of what he was wearing. Or rather what he wasn't wearing. He had on a pair of boxers and that was it. Her head lay against his bare shoulder and she had a bird's-eye view of his magnificent chest and flat abs. His powerful thighs thrust out before him were a pleasure to look at and she knew what lay beneath those boxers was just as enticing.

'Finished?' Luca asked.

Rilla's gaze pulled away from his crotch guiltily, before she realised he was asking her if she was done with the toilet. Her heart slammed in her chest and she felt like her entire body was bounding to its beat. She nodded, not trusting herself to speak.

'Come on, then,' Luca said, helping her to her feet. 'Go back to bed. I'll bring you something to eat.'

'Oh, no, Luca, I'm not sure I can eat anything,' she protested as she leaned heavily against him.

'Hey,' Luca said looking down at her. 'Tea and dry toast. Pregnant women swear by it.'

Rilla saw the look of determination in his gaze and was mesmerised by the old Luca she saw there. The one she'd fallen in love with. Before he'd withdrawn. Before the distance. She nodded. It wouldn't hurt to try, would it? And if it helped the morning sickness, she was willing to give anything a go.

Rilla crawled into bed and shut her eyes, letting the glorious ecstasy of feeling normal swamp her. She was still a bit shaky but the nausea was gone.

'Here you are,' Luca announced ten minutes later.

Rilla opened her eyes to find him bearing a tray. He'd put a shirt on, for which she was both pleased and perversely disappointed. He placed it on the bed and sat down beside it.

She eyed the dry toast dubiously but took a nibble at Luca's insistent nod. She took a sip of the sweet milky tea and was surprised to feel the fine trembling of her hands settle almost immediately.

'You're not going to work today,' Luca said, eyeing her as he bit into a crumbly croissant.

Rilla coveted the divine-smelling pastry but doubted whether her delicate system was up to it. 'Of course I am,' she said, taking another nibble of toast. 'I feel better already.'

'You don't want to overdo it,' Luca lectured.

'Luca, I could very well be sick the entire

pregnancy.' Rilla paused, horrified at the prospect. 'I can't take every day off work because of it. Plenty of women have to manage morning sickness with their work responsibilities. And now the NUM position is mine, I have to lead by example.'

Luca stopped chewing. 'You got the job?'

Rilla grinned at him and nodded. 'Yesterday was a big-news day.'

'Oh, that's fantastic, Rilla,' Luca enthused. He placed the croissant back on the plate and pulled her towards him for a quick congratulatory peck on each cheek. He knew how long she'd been after that job. After the miscarriage, after they'd drifted apart, it had become her sole focus. 'Why didn't you say something?'

Rilla lost the thread of the conversation for a moment as her senses took leave, due to his European-style, completely asexual kiss. She blinked and picked up the thread again.

'To be perfectly honest, I felt so rough and then with everything else that happened last night, it completely slipped my mind.'

Luca grinned back. 'Fair enough.'

They munched at their breakfast for a few more moments. 'Will being pregnant make a difference to getting the job?' he asked.

Rilla shrugged. She wouldn't have thought so but, then, she hadn't really had a chance to consider it. 'They've offered it to me. They can't un-offer it because I'm having a baby.'

Luca nodded. He thought about how hard she'd been working the last month and felt a niggle of worry.

'You will take it easy, wont you? The NUM job is going to be really stressful. I don't want... I'd hate for...' Luca struggled to find the right words without apportioning blame or placing guilt. They'd both done more than enough of that last time.

He ran a hand through his hair. 'I don't think I could go through another miscarriage.'

And she could? She looked into his worried gaze. 'Working had nothing to do with last time, Luca,' she said gently.

Neither had her insistence that she was perfectly capable of filling the car with petrol or persuading a reluctant Luca to make love just hours before she'd started cramping. But in the aftermath they'd dissected every little thing they had done and not done, searching for a meaning to it all.

And when they hadn't been able to find one, their individual guilt had driven them apart and they'd sought solace in their work instead of each other. Maybe seven years down the track it would be possible to forgive themselves and start anew.

Rilla placed her hand over his. 'I think it's time we both acknowledged it was something that happened that was beyond our control. That one in four pregnancies ends that way.'

Luca looked down at her hand on his. Of course she was right. Medically, he couldn't fault her. But a part of him, the Latin male part of him, would always feel he'd been tardy in his job to protect her. To protect his child.

He'd sworn as a boy growing up with an absent father that he would always be there for his child. And yet, when it had mattered, he hadn't been able to protect them. He had failed.

'I know. I was wrong to pull away from you. It was hard…harder than I ever thought. I didn't know what to do or say to you. Work was easier,' he admitted.

Rilla blinked, not expecting such frankness. Why hadn't he been able to say this to her back then? When their love had still been salvageable. Seven years of silence had inflicted more damage on their relationship than frosty communication or outright war.

'We both made mistakes, Luca,' she sighed, releasing his hand. 'We rushed into everything. Sex, living together, marriage. We didn't spend time getting to know each other, building a foundation that could take such a big hit so early in the piece.'

She picked up her toast and took a few nibbles. Luca watched her as she sipped at her tea. He picked his croissant up too and then put it down uneaten, wiping the flakes off his fingers.

He cleared his throat nervously. He'd lain awake most of the night, going over and over the situation. He'd forged a plan. It was crazy and he had no idea if she'd go along with it, but if they worked at it, it could be better than it ever had been.

'I was thinking last night…about the future…about the baby…about us.'

Rilla glanced at him warily through her fringe. Her heart did a silly flutter at his mention of 'us' but she paid it no heed. 'Oh, yes?' she said carefully.

Luca nodded and took a deep breath before he plunged on. 'I think we should reconcile. Rip up the divorce papers.'

'I…I beg your pardon?' she spluttered. She must have misheard. Reconcile? This was completely out of left field.

Luca nodded, fully prepared to take advantage of her obvious shocked state to press his case. 'Think about it. It makes sense, Rilla. You're pregnant and we're still married.'

'Officially, yes,' she said. 'But in every other way, no.'

'I'm not talking about going back to the way it was before. I'm talking about a platonic arrangement. Where we get to both be parents to our child without all the other stuff that made us so crazy before.'

Rilla gaped some more. Had he lost his mind? 'Luca…this is madness.'

'No.' Luca rose and prowled around the room.

'This is probably the most sensible thing we've ever done. Last time it was all about us. Rushing in and loving and wanting and needing and not having room for anyone or anything else. This way we start on the right foot. A focus on something else other than us. On the baby.'

'But aren't we just rushing into this?' Rilla felt completely poleaxed.

'No,' he denied. 'We're just taking the first step toward the best future for our baby. It seems hasty because it's a big step, but once we've made it we'll have months to slow down and work out the details.'

'We don't need to reconcile to do that, Luca. We just need to commit ourselves to making the baby our priority.'

'No!' Luca said, immediately rejecting her suggestion. 'I grew up with a father who was rarely around. I will not be a distant relation in my child's life.'

Rilla heard the zeal in his voice and wanted to reach out and touch him as the shadows of his childhood haunted his gaze. She knew so little about his formative years.

'I want to be part of my baby's life right from the start. See it grow inside you, every day. See every change in your body, feel every kick, be there when you go into labour. And I want to live with him or her, not down the road or around the corner. Be in its life every day. I imagine you do as well.'

'Of course,' she agreed quickly.

'Good, then this is the perfect situation for both of us. This way we get to give the baby a stable home. Two parents, living together under the same roof, that love him or her unconditionally.'

'Even if they don't love each other?'

How could she do as he was suggesting? Live under the same roof as Luca? Playing happy families when the reality would be very different? How could she live a lie?

Luca stopped pacing. 'Love? After us, I swore to myself I'd never leave my heart open for that kind of hurt again, and I meant it. It'd be especially foolish to repeat past mistakes.'

Rilla tried not to flinch but his words did make sense. What they'd had was over. Dead. She wouldn't describe either of them as gluttons for punishment.

'This is about our baby, Rilla. Just the baby.'

'You could commit to a loveless union? A marriage that's in name only? A farce?'

She made it sound so cold. So calculated. Yet it had all sounded perfectly reasonable in his head last night. Sure, he'd expected her to resist, but not over the issue of love. He wasn't sure what that meant.

'Of course. For my child, of course. Why? Are you telling me you still have feelings for me?'

Feelings for him? Not unless he counted the growing urge to slap his face. 'I'd be especially foolish to do that again,' she said mimicking him.

Touché. 'Look, Rilla,' he said, sitting on the bed and picking up her hands. They felt cold and he rubbed them absently. 'The whole love thing didn't work so well for us first time around. Maybe this is a much better way to run a marriage.'

Rilla looked into his earnest eyes. Maybe he was right. 'I don't know, Luca.'

He could see she was wavering and he scrambled his thoughts together to close the deal. Something inside him told him they could make it work. Nagged at him to make it happen.

'I do. I know we can make a success of this. We can redefine what a marriage is, Rilla. We've got months before the baby is born. Let's take the time to get to know each other.'

Rilla almost blushed, thinking about how well he knew her. She pulled her hands from his. 'I think you know me, pretty well, Luca.'

She was right. Last time there probably hadn't been one thing he hadn't known about her body. He'd known intimately the weight of her breasts in his palms, how vocal she was when an orgasm took hold of her body and exactly what to do to make her moan, to make her gasp and to make her beg.

But that wasn't what he'd meant. 'No. Let's not do what we did last time. Depend on a physical relationship to get us through. Let's spend the next eight months talking. Just talking.'

Rilla liked the sound of it. It would be good

really getting to know the man she'd married in such a rush seven years ago. What made him tick. What made him the man he was today. What had happened in his childhood to make him so adamant that he wanted to be part of his child's life that he'd float reconciliation in an all-but-dead marriage.

'We might even become friends,' Luca continued. 'Like in the old days. When we first met. Do you remember that?'

How could she not, especially with him sitting this close, his muscular thigh brushing her leg? The banter. The flirting. The tingle of anticipation. Surely he hadn't forgotten they'd moved from friends to lovers pretty quickly? 'You used to laugh, Luca,' she said softly. 'You used to laugh a lot.'

Luca took in her beautiful face, the urge to kiss the beauty spot at the corner of her mouth almost overwhelming. He lifted his hand and brushed his thumb over it instead. 'Hasn't been a whole lot to laugh about the last seven years.'

Rilla's head spun. His proximity made it hard to think straight at all. She closed her eyes as the gentle brush of his finger tingled through her entire body. She could feel her nipples tighten.

She opened her eyes slowly and stared at his perfect mouth and white teeth. 'What about sex?'

Luca's thumb stopped its impulsive caress and he dropped his hand back into his lap. He could see the tight points of her nipples outlined in his T-shirt and was pleased he'd donned a shirt to cover the ruckus that was currently going on in his boxers.

He swallowed. 'What about it?'

'Well, would there be…? Would you…? Would there be…conjugal privileges?'

Luca grinned at the frown that appeared between her eyes as she'd sought the right phrase. 'I think we need to keep this strictly platonic,' he said, sobering. 'Separate bedrooms. We've done the sex thing before and look where that got us. It'll just ruin our focus.'

Rilla couldn't believe how matter-of-fact, how analytical he sounded. 'Do you seriously think we can live under the same roof and not succumb to this crazy thing that's always been between us? Our relationship may be over but I think we've proved more than adequately that we're still sexually attracted to each other.'

Luca beat back the images from their passionate reunion. 'I think it would be a mistake,' he said stiffly. 'Do you remember what happened the last time we had sex when you were pregnant? I'm not repeating that mistake.'

A nerve jumped at the angle of Luca's jaw. Rilla could see it through the heavy overnight stubble. His voice brooked no argument. 'It wasn't that, Luca. I didn't miscarry because of that.'

Rationally, Luca knew that. He was a doctor. But he'd second-guessed everything ad nauseam from that terrible time and he wasn't prepared to risk anything this time round. 'I'm not taking any chances,' he said firmly, looking her straight in the eye.

How could he be so certain? Oh, sure, she knew all about his stubborn Latin male streak, but their still seething sexual attraction seemed to have a life of its own. Eight months of living under the same roof as Luca, married to all intents and purposes, and he really thought it could be platonic?

'Well, what do you think?' Luca probed after she'd been silent for a few moments.

What did she think? *This whole plan was stark, raving crazy.* That's what she thought. 'I think going into marriage again, even for something as noble as our child when we still have so much baggage and without love, is doomed to failure.'

Rilla wasn't sure if it was the emotionless topic or the baby but she suddenly felt violently ill. She passed her mug to Luca and bolted from the bed. She made it to the toilet just in time, her measly amount of tea and toast ejected from her stomach.

After there was nothing left to bring up Rilla sat on the bathroom floor, feeling emptier than her stomach. Luca hadn't joined her and the chill of the tiles seeped into her body. Into her bones. She shivered, pulling her knees up, dragging Luca's shirt down over them, hoping her body warmth would ward off the sudden bleakness.

She was pregnant with a much longed-for baby. It should be the happiest time of her life. But she was sick and miserable. Utterly miserable. The urge to cry welled up inside her and Rilla roused herself, refusing to sink into the abyss of self-pity again.

Feeling sorry for herself would not take the nausea away and would not help her with the Luca situation. He was no doubt pacing in her room, waiting for her decision.

She washed her face with some water, her hand trembling slightly, and brushed her teeth. She looked at herself in the bathroom mirror and knew she wouldn't be going to work today. Luca was right—she didn't look well. All she wanted to do was crawl back into bed and pull the covers over her head until the baby was ready to be born. Not even the joy of her new position could rouse her interest.

Luca was on the phone when she left the bathroom.

'I'm ringing Julia to let them know you won't be in today,' he said briskly.

She gave him a weary nod as she passed, too

tired and sick, both physically and emotionally, to care. She stood in the doorway, looking back over her shoulder at him as he spoke into the phone. Julia must have said something funny because Luca laughed. The tanned column of his neck stretched as his head flopped back against the wall.

She should have been cranky that he was taking over her life. But she wasn't. She should have cared that Julia would be wondering why Luca was calling in sick for her. But she didn't. His physique was totally distracting.

The sun filtered through the wooden blinds in the lounge room and striped his body in golden light. The grey cotton shirt clung to his contours, as did the boxers, moulding his powerful thighs. He had one leg bent up, his foot flat on the wall, and Rilla admired the shape of his knee and the manly covering of dark hair.

She dragged her gaze away and moved into the room, sinking down onto the bed. Luca had offered her a very reasonable solution to the baby situation. A reconciliation to give their baby the best option. A mother and a father living together under the same roof.

Only she wasn't so sure such things should be entered into with such a lack of emotion. It seemed fraught with potential disaster. Their relationship scars from seven years ago still needled beneath the surface. Were they just leaving themselves open for more?

But it was no use. Deep down she knew she'd do it, despite all the reasons not to. *Of course she could. Of course she would.* Because this wasn't about them. It was about their baby. And she'd do whatever it took to give it the best of everything.

She just needed to look at it as Luca did. Take herself and Luca out of the equation. Make it about the baby. Could she re-enter a stone-cold relationship for this baby? Of course she could. Like millions of women before her, she would put this child's needs first. And Luca was right—their baby deserved two parents.

'Julia said to take care and not to come back until you're feeling better.'

Rilla looked up at Luca standing in the

doorway, interrupting her train of thought. 'You didn't tell her, did you? About the baby?'

'No,' he said casually. 'Would it have been so bad if I had?'

Rilla breathed a sigh of relief. 'No, of course not. I just thought we'd wait for a bit, that's all.'

She didn't want to say, *In case I have another miscarriage.* She didn't want to tempt fate. But it was a valid point. A dreadful one, sure, but entirely valid.

Rilla remembered how awful it had been last time, having to tell the people who'd known about the pregnancy that she'd lost the baby. Deflecting questions from people who hadn't known, reliving the whole awful experience again and again as they'd apologised profusely.

Luca had avoided all the questions, walking around with a constant don't-even-think-of-talking-to-me snarl on his face, throwing himself into his work, leaving her to face the multitudes. His lack of support had added to her burden and people's well-meant concern had been like a constant rub of salt into her very raw wounds.

'Until twelve weeks?' he asked.

Rilla nodded. Entering the second trimester was an accepted milestone when the greatest miscarriage risk had passed. She'd lost the baby at eleven weeks last time.

'I can have an ultrasound then and we can start to tell people. I'm just not sure what this will mean for the NUM job. I'd rather wait…be sure…before I let Julia know. The department will have to find someone to cover me for maternity leave. They may even want to appoint two of us to job-share the role when I'm ready to come back to work.'

Luca blinked. 'You've obviously thought about this.'

'Not really, just thinking out loud.' Rilla's mind ran over all the possibilities as they spoke.

'So you plan on going back to work afterwards?'

Rilla narrowed her eyes, not fooled by his casual question. 'Yes, Luca. You know my career is important to me. You know NUM has always been my goal. At some stage I'm going to want to pick up my career. I've worked too hard and too long to ditch it altogether.'

'You want it all?'

His voice was flat and Rilla knew he didn't mean it to sound like a criticism but it did. 'Yes, Luca. Like you. Like a man. A career and a family. Why not?'

Luca ran a hand through his hair. She was right, of course, men were able to have it all. But that was a philosophical debate for another time. It was wrong and unfair but unfortunately that was largely the way it still was.

'Because it never works out like that in the real world,' he said, his voice flat.

Rilla nodded. He was right—she'd seen it so many times with her female colleagues. 'Well, I want to give it a whirl, Luca. I'm not talking about full-time work here, certainly not for a long while anyway. And I know that may require compromise with the NUM role and it may end up that I'll have bitten off more than I can chew. But I will want to return to part-time work. And later…who knows?'

'But you don't *have* to,' Luca stressed, worried that Rilla was oversimplifying and setting herself up for a lifetime of spreading herself too thinly. Like his mother had. 'I can look after you and the baby.'

'I know.' His black eyes were earnest and she could see it was important to him for her to know that.

Rilla didn't know much about his childhood but it was obvious he'd felt his own father had been remiss in his responsibilities. 'But I *want* to. I'm going to need your support, though, Luca. I can't do it without you. Do I have it?'

'You really want to go back to work after the baby's born?'

'Eventually, yes. I really do. That's a deal breaker, Luca. I'm not entering into this crazy reconciliation unless I have your word that you'll support me.'

Luca felt the first flutter of hope in his chest. She was sitting on the bed cross-legged, wearing his T-shirt and his underwear and carrying his child, and she looked pale and tired, and he knew that was to his advantage but he also knew he'd agree to almost anything.

He also knew, much to his regret, that he still wanted her. Her hair fell in thick disorder

174 DR ROMANO'S CHRISTMAS BABY

around her face and her long lashes drew him into the enticing amber trap of her eyes. The fascinating freckle at the corner of her mouth inevitably drew his gaze to the softness of her lips.

His shirt chose that moment to slip off a shoulder and he tracked the ridge of her collarbone, his eyes drawn south to the way the cotton pulled taut across her braless chest, her nipples puckering beneath his gaze. Memories of how he had ravaged them a month ago returned, and his mouth watered.

Luca cleared his throat and tried to concentrate on the negotiations. 'So you are agreeing to the reconciliation?'

'If you agree to me returning to work.'

Her gaze glowed with conviction and he actually felt that if anyone could juggle motherhood and work, she could. 'Of course,' he murmured, his gaze slipping to her mouth, the freckle enticing. 'You have my full support.'

Rilla felt the heat of his gaze and felt her nipples tighten further. Was it her hormonal state or did it feel hot in here suddenly? She tucked her knees under her chin, pulling Luca's shirt down over them. This was a serious conversation and aroused nipples had no part to play. Even so, the feel of them squashed against her warm thighs didn't ease the ache.

'Thank you,' she said, her breath annoyingly ragged.

Luca relaxed against the doorframe, his tense muscles smoothing out. 'Can you move in immediately? Today, if possible?'

Rilla blinked. 'Whoa! I thought we'd learned the not-rushing-in lesson.'

'Please, Rilla, I don't want to miss out on one day of the pregnancy.'

She sighed, completely undone by his emotive plea. She nodded slowly. What was the point in delaying any further now she'd agreed? She didn't have the right or the heart to deny Luca the connection he craved with their baby.

'I'll make some arrangements later on when I'm feeling better.'

Luca put his hand on his heart. 'Thank you, Rilla. You have made me a very happy man.'

He looked so sexy, so…Italian, standing there

in his clingy pyjamas with joy shining from his black eyes, that she practically swooned. 'Yeah, well, don't thank me yet. Just because I'm moving back, it doesn't mean we won't have our teething problems. Seven years of silence, Luca. That's a long time. I think it'll take a while to feel natural around each other again.'

Luca nodded. 'Of course. But I promise to do my best to ease the way. Our baby deserves that commitment. We can make it work for the baby's sake.'

Rilla swallowed. *For the baby.* She had to keep her eye on the ball. There was no room to be sentimental. She was reconciling with her estranged husband for definite reasons. It would be dangerous to read any more into it than that.

'I have to get ready for work,' Luca said, fighting the urge to go in and sit back on the bed beside her and seal their deal with a kiss.

Rilla nodded slowly. Somehow agreeing to a reconciliation with him standing in the doorway to her bedroom didn't seem right. It was a huge step and the distance between them made it seem like an even colder-blooded decision. But it did represent their new life together. Married without intimacy. Together for their child only. Separate bedrooms.

'Sure. I guess I'll see you tonight?'

Luca smiled. 'Tonight.' He liked the sound of that.

Coming home to Rilla.

Again.

CHAPTER SEVEN

'JINGLE Bell Rock' played quietly over the audio system as Luca watched Rilla hang tinsel along the curtain tracks of each cubicle. Of course, he was supposed to be taking advantage of the early morning lull to be reviewing some charts but she was laughing with Emily, the ward clerk, and being very distracting. He grunted to himself and returned his attention to the words in front of him.

They'd been living together for six weeks now.

Six. Very. Long. Weeks.

Six weeks of her lotions and potions cluttering the bathroom and her perfume invading every nook and cranny. Six weeks of making her tea and toast before she got out of bed and holding her hair back as she threw up every morning, the curve of her neck tempting him. Six weeks of sleepy morning smiles and her underwear in his washing basket.

She laughed again and he flicked his gaze back up to see that her shirt had ridden up as she threw a string of tinsel over the rail and he could see the soft curve of her waist. He knew that part of her body intimately. She was sensitive there. He remembered how she used to moan when he'd stroked his tongue along that particularly fascinating area.

Luca realised his attention had strayed again and he cursed under his breath. He was going mad. Six weeks of living with her and her…things and he wanted to touch her so badly he could hardly see straight. As if to demonstrate, the words blurred in front of him and he threw his pen down in disgust.

She'd been right. How the hell was he going to get through months of not touching her when only six weeks in, all he could think about was kissing her? Feeling her beneath him. For God's sake, she walked around in next to nothing at home and slept practically naked in the oppressive summer heat. Was she trying to kill him?

He picked up his pen again and forced his attention back to the charts. His mind wandered almost instantly, though, as he thought about the easy transition they'd made. Apart from the unbearable sexual tension, it had been surprisingly smooth.

If her family had been surprised, they hadn't said. They'd taken the pregnancy, the reconciliation and Rilla's move in their stride. John Winters, Rilla's father, had expressed his concern to Luca over the suddenness of it all but had been reassured by Luca's assertions that it was no frivolous, half-baked idea but a heartfelt commitment.

Hailey, who had been living at home with her parents since her return from England, had happily moved into Rilla's apartment. Everything had fallen into place. Now, if he could just banish the growing urge to touch her. To invite her into his bed. He'd seen some of the looks she'd given him from time when she'd thought he hadn't been paying attention, and he was damn sure she was feeling a little hot and bothered herself.

Not that it mattered. He'd been adamant with her from the beginning about the no-sex thing and he was sure he wasn't going to back down because Eve and her apple had moved into the room next door. Nothing was going to distract him—not her bras hanging on the line or glimpses of her damn waist—from his ultimate goal. A live, healthy newborn.

The memories from the awful day Rilla had lost the baby returned now with startling vividness. They'd made love in the early hours of the morning, when his resistance had been low. It had been over a month since they'd been intimate, a self-imposed torture, and she had rolled over and her fingers had brushed against him, his regular morning erection almost painful to touch, and whispered, 'I miss you.'

Still he had been reluctant but she'd stroked him and told him it would be OK and said, 'Please, make love to me.' And their prolonged abstinence had caused an eruption of passion and he had pinned her to the bed and thoroughly ravaged her.

Six hours later she had walked into Brisbane General, cramping and bleeding, and even though he'd known that sex during pregnancy didn't cause miscarriages, his world had been turned upside down.

'Dr Romano? Phone for you.'

Luca dragged his gaze away from Rilla and the memories, grateful for a real distraction.

Rilla was painfully aware of Luca's scrutiny as she and Emily decorated the department. Christmas in hospital was hardly anybody's idea of fun so the least they could do was make the experience a little less clinical. Rilla, a self-confessed Christmas junkie, put herself in charge of the decorations every year and it was hard to believe that the first of December had come around already.

Hard to believe that she and Luca had been co-habiting for six weeks. Sharing evening meals and early morning vomiting sessions. Washing his clothes and seeing their toothbrushes beside each other in the bathroom. It was intimate yet...not.

Luca had been true to his word. He was trying very hard to make things as natural between them as possible. Of an evening, when they were both home, they actually talked. Not about their future and how rosy it was going to be, waking up to each other every day like they had eight years ago, but about themselves. Like they should have done back then. About their likes and dislikes, their fears, their joys, their inse-curities.

And things that appeared trivial on the surface but spoke about their tastes and character. What they would grab if the house was burning down. Who they would invite to a dinner party if they could choose from anyone on the planet. What the world's most useful invention was. Which poet was better—Shelley or Byron. Was the music better in the 1970s than the 1980s?

Things that they should have known about each other already but didn't. Things they hadn't had time to talk about last time round, too caught up in lust and their rush to get down the aisle. They argued but mostly agreed and above all else they laughed. They relaxed. They had fun.

And then there was the baby—of course. They talked about the baby a lot. They made plans about the nursery and what school they wanted to enrol it in. They tossed names around and compared parenting ideas, finding themselves remarkably in tune. They even talked about getting out of the flat and buying a house so their child had a big back yard to run around in.

But there was still a reserve they'd probably never shake. She couldn't speak for him but she knew she was still protecting her heart. The miscarriage and break up had been devastating and, as he had said, they'd be foolish to put their hearts on the line again.

She'd thought his reconciliation idea had been insane to start with, but as each day went by she could see the potential. Two parents whose sole focus would be their baby. No distractions involving each other and how crazy love could make you. Cohabiting, living as a family, devoting all their love, time and attention to their child without the complication of adult love and all the potential emotional upheaval it brought to the equation.

This lead-up to the baby's birth was about re-building their relationship so when the baby finally arrived they'd both be on the same page. Actually, not so much rebuilding but restructuring. Redefining. Finding a groove that worked for them that involved mutual respect and a common purpose.

Rilla knew that would probably sound cold to some, but these days, with Luca's absolute conviction it could work, she saw it as practical. At twenty-two, she'd been young and romantic and had wanted the whole fairy-tale. As quickly as possible. But at thirty, her priorities had shifted. She just wanted the best for their baby.

'Tree now?'

Rilla blinked as Emily's voice interrupted her train of thought. 'Oh…yep,' Rilla agreed. 'The night staff assembled it for us, we just need to decorate it.'

She didn't know how long she had before her stomach would revolt again so it would be good to get it done while she was still feeling the Christmas spirit. Her morning sickness had continued unabated and it didn't seem to matter what she did or where she was, it dogged her every move. Stillness intensified it and motion aggravated it further. Smells in particular triggered crippling bouts of nausea.

They walked out to the main reception area where rows of plastic chairs sat empty, awaiting the morning rush. An eight-foot naked Christmas tree was set up near the triage desk, awaiting tinsel and baubles.

Rilla opened the box of decorations and grinned at Emily. 'Gosh, I love Christmas.'

They attacked the job with enthusiasm, singing along to the piped carols as they went. Half an hour later there was just the angel for the top left. Rilla, five feet two, looked at Emily, four feet ten, and then back up to the top of the tree.

'I don't know about you, Ems, but I don't think either of us have a chance in hell of reaching the top branch.'

Emily grinned. 'I'll get a chair.'

Emily took one of the waiting-room chairs and held it while Rilla climbed on. She rose on tiptoe and leaned forward to place the angel.

'Rilla!'

Luca's furious exclamation startled her and she toppled precariously.

'Get down from there,' he ordered, reaching her in a few angry strides and pulling her down off the seat. 'What the hell do you think you're doing?'

'I'm just hanging the angel, Luca,' she said, waving it under his nose. Her body had slid down his as he had lowered her and despite his riled expression she felt her body surge against his.

Luca saw a flare of heat in her tawny gaze and set her away from him. Inferno! *Was she deliberately trying to provoke him?* 'What if you'd fallen off the chair?' he demanded.

'Well, I nearly did, thanks to you.'

Rilla was conscious of Emily watching their heated exchange. Otherwise she would have said, *I'm pregnant, not made of glass.*

Luca's pulse rate settled now she was safely back on the floor, even if the heat in his loins hadn't. 'Give it to me,' he sighed, and held out his hand.

Rilla handed him the offending article and they watched as he barely had to stretch to ram the plastic, seen-better-days angel on the top branch. She was tacky and garish with a fluorescent red dress and a wonky halo, but the tree just wasn't dressed without her.

'She's crooked,' Emily whispered out of the side of her mouth.

Rilla bit her cheek to stop from laughing. The way he'd jammed her on the tree, it was a wonder he hadn't flattened her. 'She's crooked,' she said, returning Luca's mutinous look with an innocent smile.

'It looks fine to me,' Luca returned.

'She's crooked,' Rilla insisted.

Luca eyed the two women and grudgingly reached up to adjust the irreligious angel.

'I hope you decorate the tree at your place,' Emily whispered as they watched.

Rilla nodded. 'Doing it tonight.'

'Better?' Luca asked sardonically, turning back to the women.

Rilla and Emily, their lips pressed tightly together, nodded. 'Better. Nothing worse than a crooked angel,' Emily said.

Luca thought the angel looked like it walked

the street for eleven months of the year but wisely didn't say anything.

'Turn the lights on, Luca?' Emily asked.

Rilla put her arm around Emily's shoulders as Luca flicked the switch and the colourful lights flashed on and off, reflecting off the tinsel. A collective sigh escaped their mouths as they stared transfixed at the tree. 'Now, that's just gorgeous,' Emily said, admiring their handiwork.

'It's going to be great on night duty,' Rilla agreed. She was pleased she had a few nights rostered between now and Christmas Day.

The sliding doors interrupted their moment and they turned to see their first customer for the day. A middle-aged man holding a shirt soaked in blood to his head, accompanied by a very harried-looking woman.

'Game on,' Emily said under her breath. 'I'll get his details from the woman.'

'Thanks, Ems,' Rilla said as she ushered the man into the triage area.

Rilla was sitting in the staffroom alone, having a late lunch, when Luca tracked her down.

'It's a bit late for lunch, isn't it?' Luca frowned. 'You need to eat more regularly.'

Rilla rolled her eyes. At the moment she was a complete slave to the dictates of her stomach. 'Luca, I've snacked all morning, trying to stave off the nausea.'

He eyed her critically. She'd lost weight the last couple of weeks, her face looked leaner, her wedding ring, restored to its rightful place, was looser, and she'd complained only that morning how she needed a belt to keep her trousers up. But she had colour in her cheeks and was eating with gusto. He'd certainly seen her looking a lot worse.

'Good.' He opened the lid of his sandwich pack.

His brief, thorough examination of her made her feel like one of his patients, and she felt distinctly lacking. Her heart had been banging wildly the second he'd breezed into the room and he'd looked her up and down and dismissed her like a very uninteresting lab specimen.

She had the insane urge to stand up and strip her clothes off. Just to see how he'd react. She knew he wasn't totally immune to her, she was carrying his child after all. And she saw the way he looked at her sometimes at home when he thought she was busy doing other things. And while she hadn't deliberately courted his attention, she certainly hadn't bothered to be modest around him.

She didn't see the point. He knew her body intimately. Had seen her naked hundreds of times. And it was December in Australia, for crying out loud—too damn hot to cover up. Her night attire was a short, well-worn T-shirt and knickers. The hem of the T-shirt barely met the top of the pants but she hadn't bothered with anything more modest.

When she went to bed she discarded the T-shirt, the breeze from the ceiling fan heavenly against her heated flesh, and it certainly wasn't something she thought about putting back on again as she dashed to the toilet every morning to lose her stomach contents. Luca had taken to bringing her shirt with him to the bathroom as he checked on her.

But still she felt as if he only saw her as a vessel for his child, not as a woman any more.

He nagged her about eating well and resting and not climbing on chairs but the man who had pushed her against their front door and had his way with her seemed to have gone completely.

Which she should have welcomed, but she just couldn't switch her attraction on and off like that. Luca had always had too much sexual power over her and it seemed that seven years of bitter silence hadn't had any effect on that.

Maybe that was something else they needed to talk about, establish during the next seven months. The intimacy rules. The rules of engagement, as it were. She seriously doubted, despite Luca's apparent disinterest, whether they could live together and not cross the line at some stage. Just watching him as he ate was doing funny things to her equilibrium.

Damn it all, how could he be so…so…indifferent? Being intimate with Luca again after seven years was like a drunk having that first taste of liquor after a long period of sobriety. It was heaven and it was hell and it most definitely left her craving more.

Maybe they needed to talk about scheduling

regular intimacy time. After the baby was born. She knew better than to broach that subject with him. Maybe that way this insane itch she had could be controlled.

'Have you had a chance to talk to Julia yet?'

It took a few seconds for Rilla to realise that Luca's lips were moving because he had spoken. She'd been so deep in thought and focused on the way they moved as he ate, nothing else had registered.

'Hmm?' she asked, desperately trying to clear wanton images from her brain.

Luca felt heat slam into his groin as she lifted her tawny gaze to him. It shimmered with naked desire. 'Julia? About the baby.' He could hear the tremulous note in his voice and saw her pupils dilate a little more.

'Oh, yes. I'll pop in and see her after my shift finishes.'

Luca held her gaze. 'Don't forget. You've had the ultrasound. You agreed.'

Rilla felt the simmering sexual tension quickly dissipate. The man had a one-track mind and it had absolutely nothing to do with the inferno that had raged between them a second ago. 'Damn it, Luca. I'm not a child,' she snapped, scraping her chair back.

Luca watched her throw her wrappers in the bin and storm out of the staffroom without a backward glance. *Dio Santo!* He knew that. Her skimpy attire around the house had left him in no doubt she was most definitely, one hundred per cent all woman.

She forgot her antipathy towards Luca as the department quickly turned into Bedlam central. There seemed to be a vomiting and diarrhoea bug going around and most of the cubicles were filled with patients, from babies through to the elderly, in varying stages of dehydration.

The heat, combined with the inability to keep anything down, had taken a huge toll on the most vulnerable members of the population. IV fluids and anti-emetics were the order of the day.

She also dealt with several fractures, a minor head injury, two chest pains, a snakebite and a build-up of ear wax requiring syringing. By the time she left, she'd done three hours' overtime and was completely exhausted. Her feet ached and she wanted nothing more than to crawl into bed.

'You finally off?' Luca asked her as she walked past the central desk, bag over her arm.

Rilla nodded. 'And, yes,' she interrupted him as he opened his mouth, 'I have spoken to Julia.'

Luca grinned sheepishly. 'What'd she say?'

'She was thrilled. We're going to discuss how to tackle the NUM position over the next few days.'

Luca wanted to pick her up and swing her round but he noticed the flyaway wisps of hair that had escaped her ponytail and the way she kept shifting from foot to foot. She looked done in and he wanted to gather her close and rub her shoulders.

'You're tired. I hope you're going to lie down for a rest when you get home.'

Rilla rolled her eyes. 'Yes, sir.' She gave him a weary salute. 'Don't be too late tonight, we're decorating the tree, remember?' she said, stifling a yawn.

Luca nodded. 'I'll try but the Bat-phone's just

rung to give us a heads-up about a multi-vehicle accident. I could be a while.'

Rilla nodded, well used to the demands of Luca's job. 'OK. I'll wait up.'

'Rilla, you're exhausted,' Luca protested.

'It's the first,' she insisted with a smile. 'The tree has to go up on the first of December. It's the rule.'

Music interrupted their conversation and they followed the sound, making their way out to the main waiting area to discover a school choir singing 'Joy to the World'. Every year from the first of December to Christmas Day various schools and churches took turns in sending a choir to the General each evening. The choir would move from ward area to ward area, singing Christmas carols.

Rilla sighed as she drew up next to Julia, who was leaning on the triage desk. 'I love Christmas in hospital.'

'Yes,' Julia agreed. 'Aren't these kids great?'

'Superb.'

They were dressed in long red gowns and carried candles. The Christmas tree twinkled and it couldn't have been any more perfect if it had snowed. Rilla watched the stressed faces of the waiting public smooth out and their frowns turn into smiles. Even the grizzly children quietened.

The song drew to a close and the choir began 'Silent Night', followed by 'Ding, Dong, Merrily on High'.

'Where are they from?' Luca asked.

'St Barnabus's, I think,' Julia said, turning her head to acknowledge him briefly.

They listened to the carol in silence, stirring only when it ended and the choir moved on, applause following in their wake.

Rilla said her goodbyes again, then went to her old apartment, where she relieved Hailey of all the Christmas decorations she'd inherited after their marriage had broken up. She remembered how magical their first Christmas had been and how she'd gone completely nuts, buying every shiny, sparkly bauble she'd laid eyes on.

Of course, they'd only been together for three months by that time. And had spent their entire time in bed, loving the season away. But this year was going to be different. This year they would lay the traditions for future Christmases as a family.

Rilla followed Luca's orders when she finally got home, so weary all she could think of was sleep. She fell into an exhausted heap on the bed and didn't wake up for two hours.

When she rose a familiar queasy sensation sat heavily in her stomach and she dozed on and off for a while until it lifted. Luca wasn't home yet so she fixed herself a bland snack and put a Bing Crosby CD in the player. He sang about white Christmases in the sultry summer heat and Rilla hummed along. She could almost hear the sleigh bells and feel the snow against her face.

Trimming the tree at work that morning had infected her with the bug and she decided to make a start on decorating the lounge, leaving the tree for her and Luca to decorate together.

She strung tinsel around the doorways and windows and across the walls. She erected a pretty Christmas wreath of frosted berries and set up a porcelain nativity scene on top of the bookshelf. She shook the can of fake snow and frosted the windows, then placed electric candles all along the sill.

By nine o'clock she was feeling proud of her achievements. Between the tinsel and Bing, the room was looking very festive. Luca still wasn't home as Rilla pieced together the artificial tree. She wasn't worried. She knew an emergency medicine consultant could work very long hours. But she was impatient to get the tree decorated.

Luca was in a foul mood when he got home just after eleven. The multi-trauma had kept them busy for hours. Two teenage deaths, despite their best efforts, six criticals and twelve other patients with minor injuries had made for a tough night. The mound of paperwork had compounded the situation.

He threw his keys on the telephone table in the hall, jerking his tie loose. He could hear the voice of Bing Crosby drifting from the lounge. Was Rilla still up? Damn it! Surely she hadn't waited up this late? He stalked into the lounge room.

The lights were out, the room lit only by a

small glow coming from the window-sills. Luca took in the room's transformation dispassionately as his pupils adjusted to the gloom and he laid his eyes on Rilla's sleeping form sprawled out on the couch.

She was lying on her back, the leg closest to the edge bent at the knee, her foot touching the ground. The other stretched out straight. Her T-shirt had ridden up, barely covering her breasts. A hand rested carelessly on her stomach. Her midriff was bare and he could just make out her gauzy pink knickers.

The soft glow bathed her face. Her lips, slackened in slumber, looked inviting. The sexy freckle at the corner of her mouth practically beckoned him. *Damn it—no!*

He stumbled towards her. 'Rilla.' He leaned forward and shook her shoulder.

Rilla heard his voice from a distance and smiled. She liked the way his accent made her name sound full and round and sexy.

Luca saw the small smile cross her full lips. *Dio!* 'Rilla,' he said again, giving her a firmer shake.

'What? I'm awake, I'm awake,' Rilla spluttered, jackknifing into a sitting position as the tendrils of an elusive dream flowed out of reach.

'Go to bed. That couch will kill your back.' God knew, he'd had way too much personal experience with it. In the last few weeks of their marriage it had been his bed.

Rilla smiled up at him. 'You're back.'

Luca felt his heart in his mouth at the look of serene pleasure she gave him. Not sexual pleasure, just plain, unadulterated happy to see you.

'Yes,' he agreed tiredly. 'It's late, go to bed.'

'Is it still the first?' she asked sleepily.

He smiled, her slow blinking amber eyes mesmerising. 'Yes, for another fifty minutes.'

'Good.' Rilla laughed, sleep still dulling her perception. 'Look at the room, Luca!' she exclaimed, rising from the couch, still entranced by its magic. 'Aren't the candles pretty?'

Luca should have been looking at the candles. At that moment he was struggling for any distraction from her legs or the way her T-shirt slid enticingly across her chest. Candles were a good option. 'Very nice,' he said, still not looking at the candles.

Rilla was more awake now and despite the subdued light was homing in on his mood. 'Luca?'

'Rilla, please.' He was tired. Too tired to resist her sleepy mouth and skimpy clothes.

'It was bad, wasn't it? The multi-trauma?'

Luca sighed, knowing his sudden irritability didn't have a whole lot to do with work but also knowing that telling two sets of parents their teenagers were dead hadn't helped. 'Yes, it was bad.'

He was so still. She knew he'd never liked talking about the tragedies that happened at work but tonight especially, the night they were going to decorate their tree, she couldn't bear the thought of him hurting.

'I have just the antidote,' she murmured as she turned on her heel, went into the kitchen and cracked the lid on a long-necked beer.

She walked back towards him, trying not to be affected by how sexy he looked in the muted light. She stopped a hand's breadth away from him and pushed the beer at his chest with one hand as she reached up and pulled the loosened knot on his tie with the other, relieving him of it. 'The tree still needs trimming.'

Luca took the beer and prayed for restraint. His heart thudded like a drum in his chest. Surely she could hear it? 'It's late,' he protested half-heartedly.

'It's still the first,' she insisted quietly.

Luca took a step back. A step away from her intoxicating presence. In the half-light she was even more desirable. 'You're incorrigible,' he sighed, taking a swig of his beer.

Rilla clapped her hands gleefully, knowing she'd won. 'Bah, humbug,' she said dismissively as she opened the box of decorations.

Together they decorated the tree. Luca placed the lights first and then they added the bells and the tinsel. Rilla hummed along to Bing while Luca smiled at her as he drank his beer.

'Tell me about Christmas in Italy,' she said as she handed him one of the two dozen fine glass snowflakes Beth had bought in London when she had lived in England.

Luca made her smile and laugh with his child-hood anecdotes. He mentioned his father quite a bit and Rilla felt it was her best opening to push him a little more. They'd done a lot of talking over the last six weeks but he'd always shied away from his childhood.

'It sounds like you have some pretty good memories of your dad too,' she said gently.

Luca didn't answer straight away, although she could sense his turmoil. She kept hanging ornaments and waiting, hoping he'd open up.

When he finally did answer Rilla was startled at his voice. He'd been silent for so long she'd thought maybe he hadn't heard her.

'My father was…a drifter. A dreamer. Always had some harebrained scheme on the boil. Always traveling around the countryside, trying to sell it to someone, looking for a backer.'

Rilla heard love, pride and exasperation in equal measure. She'd never met Santo Romano, who had died when Luca had been fifteen, but it was clear that conflicting emotions warred inside Luca.

'He was never home and didn't really have any

kind of regular employment. Money was tight but Mamma…she was determined that we wouldn't be disadvantaged. She took in laundry and ironing, as well as working in the *latteria* during the day and my grandfather's *ristorante* at night.'

Rilla could well believe Luca's mother being the driving force in the family. She had met Maria Romano on their Italian honeymoon, and even in her sixties there'd been a steely determination in the matriarch's demeanour.

'And still she was there for us all before school, after school, before bed. But she was always exhausted and thin, so thin. No time to eat or look after herself properly. She never said anything but I could see the envy in her eyes when she saw the other mothers in the park with their kids.'

Rilla could see Luca had gone back to another time in a far-away land and she daren't say a word for fear he might never talk about it again.

'I heard her and my father arguing once after he'd come back from being away for months. She was saying she just wanted to have time for us to go to the park.'

Rilla watched Luca rouse himself, raising the bottle to his lips and taking another swallow. He turned to her. 'I wished we could have gone to the park too.' He gave a self-deprecating laugh. 'Selfish, huh?'

Rilla's heart felt heavy and her arms ached to embrace the wounded little boy that lay beneath the strong, capable doctor. She touched his arm. 'You were a child, Luca.'

Luca nodded. 'I don't want that for you. For my wife. Or for my child.'

Her entire body bounded with the slow, hard thump of her heart. So this whole going-back-to-work thing was Luca's desire to look after and provide for her and their baby. To make up for his own father's shortcomings. To be the man his father hadn't been. To save her from becoming his mother.

Rilla took some deep steadying breaths, trying to dispel the emotion she knew would make her voice husky. 'Why didn't you ever tell me this before?'

Luca shrugged. 'I don't guess we did do a whole lot of talking the first time around.'

No, they hadn't. Their love had spiralled out of control around them, catching them up in a whirlwind of lust and desire, whipping all notions of a sensible courtship into the stratosphere. All they'd wanted had been to be together.

'Not really. We never really discussed having children, did we?' she ventured.

Luca shrugged. He couldn't recall if they had. He'd always been too interested in the process that made babies. They both had, if he recalled correctly. And yet they'd got married and hadn't ever discussed something as important as a family? What fools they'd been.

She was excruciatingly conscious of him beside her, not moving, staring at the Christmas tree, wrapping a scrap of tinsel around his hand.

'Just this to go,' she said, holding up the angel. 'Unless you want me to get up on a chair…'

Luca whipped the angel from her and smiled. 'Very funny.'

He placed it on top and then the tree was complete. Rilla switched out the main lights and flicked on the tree lights. The colourful display sent rainbows around the room, glowing on the walls as it reflected off red tinsel and snowflakes.

She sat back on the sofa and snuggled into the leather, feasting her eyes on the beauty, letting the music and the tree weave their Christmas magic.

'Come and look, Luca.' She sat, patting the lounge beside her. 'Isn't it beautiful?'

Luca nodded, sitting reluctantly beside her. As far as he was concerned, her beauty outshone the tree by far. He didn't dare look at her—in fact, he daren't even breathe. He could already smell her shampoo.

Eight years ago he'd have placed his hand on her thigh, tucked her head beneath his chin, stroked his finger down her bare arm. Eight years ago he'd have had her naked and under him in moments. He stood abruptly, removing himself from the exquisite torture of her nearness.

Rilla looked up, surprised at his hasty with-drawal. It had been cosy, watching the tree with him. Obviously the multi-trauma had been a lot worse than he was letting on.

'Sit, Luca,' she murmured, reaching for his

arm. As someone who had worked side by side with Luca during too many awful traumas, she understood his state of mind. 'I'll get you another beer.'

Luca sat, grateful she'd moved out of his orbit and he could breathe again. He shut his eyes and relaxed back into the soft cushions. It had been a long day and talking about his parents, on top of two dead teenagers and Rilla in her under-wear, had taken its toll.

Rilla lingered in the doorway, her gaze drawn to Luca. His shirt was untucked and he'd loosened the top buttons of his shirt. He looked tired and defeated and it roused all her female instincts. She wanted nothing more than to go and rub his shoulders. Help him out of his shirt. Press kisses to his chest. See his beautiful lips soften into that knowing sexy smile.

Help! Why did she still want him so much?

'Here,' she said quietly, holding the bottle out to him, watching as his eyes cracked open and he roused himself to take it.

She sat beside him again, her gaze returning to the tree. She sighed contentedly. This was great. Maybe this whole crazy idea of Luca's really could work.

Luca couldn't resist looking down at her. He could see the coloured lights reflected in her amber eyes, gilding them in different shades of gold. She looked up at him and smiled and her lips were soft and moist and he almost groaned he wanted to kiss her so badly.

Rilla's lips tingled as his gaze lingered and she couldn't look away. 'Thank you,' she whispered, 'for doing the tree with me.' And on sheer impulse she leaned forward and dropped a brief kiss against his mouth.

Luca pulled back quickly, as if she'd bitten him, and Rilla couldn't stop the shaft of disappointment piercing the warm glow inside. 'Oh, sorry… Old habits…'

Luca regarded her from between lowered lids as he sought to get control of the heat that coursed through his body. He watched her mouth as she said something else and he muttered an oath as he cupped his hand around the nape of her neck and pulled her lips back to his.

Dio! He didn't want this but her lips felt

perfect beneath his and as he explored her mouth with his tongue, she tasted so good he never wanted to stop. Her moan went straight to his groin and he cupped her face as he deepened the kiss, pushing her back into the sofa.

He could hear her tremulous breathing as she fought to match his ardour and he growled low in his throat as she gripped the front of his shirt, knowing that he was making her breathless and needy. She whimpered as he laved her lips with long slow strokes from his tongue and he felt his control completely snap when she let out a frustrated 'Luca.'

His hand swept down her side, lingering at the swell of her breast and gripping her hip. A surge of possession swamped him, knowing their child lay nestled nearby, and he pulled her hard against him.

Her sharp gasp was like a bucket of cold water. *Dio!* She was pregnant with his child and he was yanking her around like a rag doll! 'What?' Luca demanded, pulling away, his eyes roving over her body, inspecting her. 'Did I hurt you?'

Rilla lay dazed, desperately groping around for her scattered thoughts. 'No, of course not,' she said, half sitting, her body aching with desire so rampant she wanted to drag him back down again, but she could tell as she watched him get up from the couch that the moment had passed. 'It was… I was…caught up in the moment… I'm fine.'

Luca ran a frustrated hand through his hair. Rilla was lying all rumpled against the sofa and he needed to get out of the room—now. How could he have lost control so easily? 'I'm sorry. That won't happen again,' he muttered.

Oh, God, she hoped not. 'I'm fine, Luca,' she repeated.

He braved a look at her and wished he hadn't. God help him, he wanted to drag her to his room. By her hair, if necessary, although the way she was looking at him he doubted whether she'd fight him. 'Goodnight.' He turned and stalked from the room.

Rilla fell back against the couch, still trying to normalise her breathing, the ache between her legs unbearable.

She glared after him, looking at nothing but empty space.

Come back and finish what you started, damn it.

CHAPTER EIGHT

THEY both pretended the kiss hadn't happened and things settled back into a routine. They'd go to sleep in their separate rooms, he'd join her in the bathroom as she threw up each morning and then make her dry toast and tea for breakfast. They went to work. And so it went on.

And before Rilla knew it, two weeks had sped by and she was fourteen weeks pregnant and feeling more and more confident. The pregnancy was progressing well and the morning sickness was showing signs of abating.

She pulled her car into a parking space at the General in time for her late shift and hummed all the way to the staffroom. A small Christmas tree, about a third of the size of the one in the waiting room, stood in the corner. It was laden with 'secret Santa' presents, and Rilla smiled as she added hers to the large pile on the floor under the tree.

She'd drawn Julia's name and had found an exquisite hand-blown glass bauble at the Southbank Christmas markets. Rilla had spent way more than the requisite ten dollars but she hadn't been able to resist it. Julia was a dear friend and a fantastic boss who hadn't blinked when Rilla's unexpected pregnancy had thrown a spanner in the works. She deserved a little something extra. And it was Christmas!

She hunted around the tree, unable to resist looking for her own present, locating it right down the bottom. She puzzled over the handwriting and had a good feel of the soft package, feeling a little thrill of excitement. God, she loved Christmas. And this one with Luca back in her life and the baby was extra-special.

'Hah! Caught you,' Julia crowed as she bustled into the staffroom.

'Guilty,' Rilla grinned, replacing her present. 'I was just having a feel.'

'What are you and Luca doing on Christmas Day?'

'We're going to Mum and Dad's for lunch.

Everyone will be there. Even David and his fiancée.'

'Oh, it's great that David's going to be joining you all. Beth must be so happy, having both her kids together this year. Especially after the fright with Bridie. Hope he doesn't find the Winters clan too full on.'

Rilla laughed. 'We can be a bit over the top. Especially at Christmas. I think he's getting used to us and I'm pretty sure Beth's warned him.'

Julia smiled. 'Come on, then, I'll give you a quick handover.'

'Hang on,' Rilla stalled, giving her present one last feel.

'You're incorrigible.' Julia laughed, shaking her head.

Julia was right, she *was* incorrigible. But nothing could dampen her Christmas spirits. Too many Christmases the last seven years had reminded her of what she hadn't had any more and this year things finally felt right.

All the patients got a special Christmas greeting and an extra hundred watts in her smile. Sitting in an emergency department was never fun but was even less so at Christmas, so Rilla went all out to make their time as jolly as she could.

She saw Luca quite a bit as she hummed her way through her shift. He laughed at her elf hat and her brooch that lit up and played 'Jingle Bells' whenever anyone touched it.

Seven o'clock came round and miraculously the workload was bearable and Rilla got to witness one of her favourite events. Santa's visit. Every Christmas, Norman, one of the orderlies, dressed up as Santa and went ho-ho-ho-ing around all the ward areas. He always seemed to find a willing sidekick to dress as an elf and they gave out sweets and balloons as they spread their Christmas cheer.

Rilla loved the tradition. She loved watching the solemn faces in the waiting room light up, if even for a few seconds. Several children sat with anxious parents and their faces were pictures as the man in the red costume and his elf spared them some time.

He passed by Rilla, who was grinning madly at the spectacle from the triage desk.

'Ho, ho, ho, Sister Winters, and a merry

Christmas to you,' Norman said, giving her a wink as he stopped to chat. 'Have you been naughty or have you been nice?'

Rilla laughed. 'Nice, of course.'

'Hmm, perhaps I should be asking your husband that. What do you reckon, Doc?'

Rilla turned to see Luca approaching.

'She's had her moments,' Luca drawled. *Trying hard to make things work—nice. Walking around in next to nothing at the flat— naughty. Kissing him—very, very naughty.*

'I think Dr Romano is telling lies, Santa. A bundle of sticks for him on Christmas morning,' Rilla said, ignoring Luca and how devastatingly handsome he looked in his business shirt, a stethoscope decorated with tinsel slung around his neck and a teasing smile hovering on his beautiful mouth.

'Oh, dear, Doc,' Norman laughed, 'think you blew that. And will there be something special in your stocking, Sister Winters?'

Rilla smiled. 'I have all I want,' she said, her hand covering her abdomen.

'Well, well, must get on,' Norman said with a

grin. 'Come on, Elf,' he bellowed, and rang his sleigh bells. 'The orthopaedic ward next.'

Luca and Rilla watched them go, the tinkle of bells resonating long after the red suit and green elf hat had disappeared from sight. Luca looked down at Rilla, her hand still placed protectively on her stomach. Her hair was tied back with a piece of tinsel and bits had escaped to fall around her face. Her cheeks glowed and her eyes danced and a smile played across her mouth. She looked like a kid let loose in a sweet shop.

'What?' Rilla asked, looking up into his intense black gaze, conscious that her voice was suddenly husky.

'Nothing.' Luca shook his head slightly. 'You just… you look beautiful tonight.'

Rilla felt her stomach lurch. When he looked at her like that, she felt beautiful.

'Bat-phone's just rung. Ambulance Control says boating accident out on the bay,' Emily said, bustling towards them, unaware she was interrupting their moment. 'First ambulance ETA ten minutes. Patient one, compound fractured tib and fib and major leg laceration from the propeller, mild hypothermia.'

Emily read rapidly from a piece of paper. 'They're just loading patient two at the scene. Critical. Near-drowning. Hypothermic. Uncertain downtime. Managed to get a rhythm.'

'Thanks, Ems,' Rilla said, removing her elf hat, her brow furrowing as her mind worked out what they'd need, anticipating any complications. 'I'll head out to Resus.'

Luca joined her at the ambulance doors a few minutes later as the siren wailed ever closer. She smiled at him, feeling jittery as the adrenaline kicked in. They snapped on gloves as the ambulance pulled to a hasty stop.

Rilla greeted the paramedic who leapt out of the vehicle and stood back while he opened the rear doors. A blanket-swathed, elderly man sat on the trolley. He hastily pulled off his oxygen mask and grabbed Rilla's hand as the trolley was unloaded and she introduced herself.

'My wife. Have you heard anything about my wife? I couldn't find her…I tried… I don't know what I'll do if anything happens to her.'

The man looked frantic. He was ashen-faced and his fingers were cold, and he clutched Rilla's hand as if he could influence the news the harder he held on. Rilla's heart went out to him and she flicked a glance at Luca. This is what real love was. A real marriage.

She remembered feeling that way about Luca in the beginning. That if anything ever happened to him, she would die. But he'd gone away and she was still here to tell the tale. What they had now seemed preferable to Stan's gut-wrenching panic.

Rilla smiled at her patient and placed the mask back on his face. 'Stan, let's get you inside and get your leg seen to, and I promise I'll let you know as soon as I hear anything, OK?'

Rilla walked alongside the trolley as Luca assisted the paramedic to push it inside. They had Stan settled on a hospital gurney within a minute and Rilla listened to the handover from the paramedic as she hooked her patient up to the monitor, placed a blood-pressure cuff around his arm and took a tympanic temperature.

'What have we got?' Luca asked, turning to her as the paramedic left.

'BP one hundred and fifty over ninety-five. Temp thirty-five.'

Luca nodded. 'Let's get some warmed Hartman's into him.' The paramedics had already inserted two large-bore cannulae. 'Some warm blankets too. How's the leg, Stan?'

Stan pulled his oxygen mask off. 'It's fine. Have you heard anything more about my wife? Please…we've been married for fifty years.'

Luca felt his gut clench as he watched Rilla replace the oxygen mask. Fifty years? He and Rilla hadn't made it past three months. The older man's desperation was palpable. 'I just need to do a couple of things here with you first then I'll go and check.'

The paramedics had bandaged Stan's lower leg and then supported it in an air splint. Rilla passed Luca a pair of scissors and he cut through the dressing. Stan's leg was far from fine. Both the smashed bones were visible through a very deep laceration that extended from his shin to his calf, splitting the bulky muscle wide open.

The wound was oozing slightly but Stan had obviously been lucky enough not to have severed any major arteries or he would have bled to death in the water.

Rilla screwed up her nose at the mangled-looking leg. 'Is it hurting, Stan?' It had to be.

Stan just shook his head, his shoulders shaking as muted sobs escaped his lips. Rilla put her hand on the man's shoulder. 'It looks like it must hurt very badly.'

Stan pushed the mask aside. 'Not as much as it hurts in here.' The older man tapped his chest.

'You have chest pain?' Luca asked, his brows drawing together.

'No, no, no,' Stan muttered. 'Are you married, Doc? Sister?'

Luca nodded. 'To each other, actually.'

Rilla glanced at Luca, surprised by this personal admission to a patient.

'Then you know,' Stan said, patting Rilla's hand. 'I don't care about my leg. I only care about my Irene.'

Luca glanced at Rilla. He wasn't sure they knew much about anything. She returned his look and he could tell she felt just as confused. How would he feel if he thought she'd drowned?

Frantic.

Of course he'd be frantic. She was the mother of his child. He dragged his gaze away from hers with difficulty.

'Well, I care about your leg, Stan, so we'll need an X-ray and an orthopaedic consult. Some morphine, too.'

'I'll get it,' Rilla said. 'I'll also find out an ETA on Irene.'

'Bless you,' Stan said from behind his mask.

Rilla was glad to escape for a moment. Being around Stan and witnessing his obvious devotion to his wife was cutting a little too close to the bone for her. It made what she and Luca had seem hollow, despite their very sensible reasoning.

By the time the second ambulance pulled up at the General twenty minutes later, Stan had been given something for his pain and, thanks to five warm blankets and warmed IV fluids, his temperature was almost back to normal. He fretted as he was wheeled to X-Ray about missing his wife's arrival.

Rilla, for one, was pleased he was away. Irene was not in good shape.

'Just lost her output again.' A paramedic was balancing on the trolley, straddling the patient and administering chest compressions as the other one pushed the trolley and hand-bagged the already intubated patient.

They stopped CPR briefly as Irene was transferred to a hospital gurney. 'Rilla, take over chest compressions,' Luca ordered as he took charge of the airway.

Rilla responded automatically, vaguely listening to the handover while Julia, who had joined them, worked around her to get Irene hooked up to the monitor.

'Temp is thirty-three,' Julia announced.

'Let's get some warm fluids running and switch the heater lamps on,' Luca ordered.

The cubicle was bathed in bright light as someone flicked the light on and Rilla felt the intense heat instantly on her hair.

Things weren't looking good for Irene but Rilla knew Luca wouldn't give up on this patient until her core temperature had normalised. Heart and brain activity slowed right down in hypothermia and that needed to be reversed before the true condition of the patient was known. The cardinal rule—a patient wasn't dead until they were warm and dead.

She paused her compressions so they could see what rhythm the monitor was showing.

'Coarse VF,' Luca said, a little cheered to see some electrical activity. Some evidence that the heartbeat was still there. A fine VF would have been a worse prognosis. The sign of a heart fading fast. Still, Irene was up against it. Only a small percentage of out-of-hospital arrests ever made it. 'Let's defib.'

Julia handed the pads to Rilla, who slapped them in place. 'Everyone clear,' Julia announced. Rilla stood back from the trolley. Luca dropped the ambu-bag and stood back also.

She pushed the button and the machine delivered one hundred joules, Irene's chest arching off the bed.

'Still VF,' Rilla said.

'Charge it to two hundred,' Luca ordered.

They shocked Irene several times and managed to get a slow junctional rhythm with a reasonable cardiac output.

'What's her temp now?' Luca asked.

'Thirty-four point five,' Rilla replied, reading it off the monitor. Julia had placed an oesophageal probe so they could assess their patient's core temperature better.

'OK. Good. Getting there.' Hopefully, as Irene warmed further her heart rate would improve.

Stan had returned from X-Ray and was now just a thin cotton curtain away. He was calling to his wife, telling her he loved her and begging her not to leave him and Rilla felt an almost desperate need for her elderly patient to make it. *Fifty years.* She didn't want to have to look into Stan's eyes and see half a century crushed into the dust.

She accompanied Luca into Stan's curtained-off cubicle a few moments later and they relayed the news. Irene was critical but her condition had stabilised.

'Oh, thank you, thank you,' Stan muttered, taking Rilla's hand, tears coursing down his cheeks. 'She's my everything. She's all I ever wanted.'

'Stan, I need you to realise there are no guarantees,' Luca emphasised. 'Irene had extended downtime, things could still go either way, and if she pulls through we have to look at the possibility that she may have sustained brain damage.'

The older man looked at him. 'I hear you, Doc. We'll cross that bridge if we get to it. I just wasn't ready for her to go. Not yet.'

Rilla nodded and let Stan talk some more. She and Luca both just listened.

'You look after this girl, Doc,' Stan said, patting Rilla's hand. 'You never know when it can all be snatched away.'

Only he did. Luca did know love could be snatched away. Eroded. Had lived through it once. He patted the older man's hand, the thought of losing Rilla again acutely unbearable. 'I will, Stan. I will.'

Rilla caught his eye and wished she could

read his thoughts. Something was there. And it didn't look very platonic.

Stan went to Theatre to have his leg fixed as Irene was being transferred to ICU, and the night got busier. Two hours later, when Rilla was due to knock off, Luca was still caught up in Resus, working on an epileptic woman who had presented via ambulance with continuous seizures. They had only just managed to bring the fitting under control.

'I shouldn't be too much longer,' Luca assured her.

She nodded. 'I'll see you at home later.'

Rilla showered and fixed herself a snack while Bing serenaded her in the background. She plunged the house into darkness and hummed along as she flicked on the tree lights. She pulled a cushion from the couch, tucking it under her head as she lay back on the carpet and stared up at the tree.

It was beautiful, and the baubles, silver bells and red tinsel reflected the light. The presents already piling up looked even more enticing, with colorful little spotlights enhancing their festive wrappers. The angel looked down at her with a serene all-is-well-with-the-world smile.

And Rilla did have a sense that all was well. She covered her stomach with her hand and almost wriggled at the thought that next year she would be sharing this experience with her baby. With Luca's baby. They both would. As a family. And that was the true meaning of Christmas. Surely?

She couldn't wait. OK, the baby would only be six months old but every year would be more wondrous than the last and Rilla just knew their child would grow up with a love for this season as deep as her own. She would see to it.

She shut her eyes and let Bing and her inner peace drift her away into a snowy moonlight field alive with sugar-plum fairies and the tinkle of sleigh bells.

It was midnight when Luca finally arrived home. He heard Bing and smiled as he shook his head. He must get Rilla another CD of carols. He stopped in the doorway, his breath stuttering to a halt in his throat. Rilla was lying on her back, asleep on the floor near the tree. Her knickers were brief, her T-shirt had ridden up and her hair lay loosely around her head in rumpled disorder. His mouth felt suddenly dry and he clenched his hands by his sides.

Dio! Was she trying to kill him?

He should go to bed. Just get the hell out of the lounge and go straight into bed. But he knew he couldn't leave her on the floor all night. Mornings weren't her best time and she didn't want to add backache to her woes.

'Rilla.' He moved closer until he was standing looking down at her. He nudged her gently with his foot.

She murmured something and rocked her head from side to side but didn't wake up. Luca sighed and hunkered down beside her. He lifted a hand to shake her shoulder but was caught by the play of colourful lights against her skin and the protective way her fingers were splayed low on her belly.

His baby lay beneath that hand. Their baby. He shook his head at the wonder of it all and gave in to the urge to lie down beside her. He lay on his side, his elbow bent, his head propped on his hand, and gazed down at her, watching her abdomen as the skin changed hue from pink to green to blue to yellow.

He had never thought he'd get a second chance at this. Never. When things had ended between them he hadn't even been able to contemplate something this wonderful ever happening again. The end had been too painful, too soul-destroying to ever want to be here again. But he was. And he wanted to hold his baby so badly he couldn't resist putting his hand out to touch her.

She murmured again as his fingers slid lightly over hers and he stilled, not wanting to disturb her. After a few moments he brushed the pad of his thumb over her wedding ring and then gently interwove their fingers to compare his wide platinum band with her narrow gold one, remembering the day they'd exchanged them.

Her skin felt warm beneath his hand and he was excruciatingly aware of the life force pulsing beneath his palm. He stroked her belly with his thumb. Released her fingers and placed his hand fully against her, absorbing the beauty of her skin and the promise of the life growing inside her.

Rilla came awake slowly, gently drifting out of the wonderful fantasy to the soft strains of music, a smile on her face. Luca's face loomed above hers and for a moment it felt like she was still caught up in the dream.

'Luca,' she murmured. 'Is it Christmas yet?'

Her mouth was so near and his gaze was drawn to it as she spoke. Luca sucked in a breath as her sleepy eyes blasted him with a heady, sultry power. 'Not yet,' he croaked.

Rilla was suddenly very much awake. Even in the subdued light she could see Luca's eyes were glittering with desire. His hand felt white hot against her stomach and she wanted to give a great feline stretch and have it move lower.

She could hear his unsteady breathing, or was that hers? She could smell the heady mix of his aftershave and something more basic and harder to pinpoint. *Pheromones.* The crispness of his business shirt grazed erotically against the bare flesh of her side and she itched to place her palms against it, undo the buttons, strip it from his chest.

Since waking up to find him watching her, his hand on her stomach, the sizzle between them had been building. *Hell, it had been building for weeks.*

Her blood pooled low in her belly and heated her breasts and it took her a beat or two to gather her scattered thoughts. She swallowed. 'Luca?'

He could hear the desperate edge to her voice and knew they were both teetering on the edge of something that involved a very long drop. Luca could feel her gaze on his mouth. His lips tingled.

His hand was still on her stomach and she was looking up at him like she used to do, like she had before he'd kissed her the other night. Reminding himself that this wasn't a real marriage was not helping.

'Rilla.'

She could hear the note of foreboding in his voice but she could also hear how strained it sounded. How achy and needy, his accent even more pronounced from the want lacing his words.

'I…I miss kissing you,' she whispered and lifted her hand to stroke her index finger along the seam of his lips.

Luca felt her husky words go straight to his groin. He swallowed. 'This isn't going to happen.'

He sat up abruptly, his legs bent up, his arms loosely slung around his knees, his hands locked together in case they decided to operate without his authority.

Rilla hissed out a pent-up breath. She was so hot she felt sure she'd combust at any second. She sat up too, their arms close, their combined breathing loud in the room. She looked at him. The reflection of the coloured lights played across the stubble on his jaw and he looked darker and more Latin than ever.

She wanted him so much her vision was just a red haze of lust, too far gone to heed any sensible thoughts of caution. 'Just kiss me, Luca. Please. Just one kiss.'

The sensible, rapidly evaporating side of Luca knew there could be no such thing as just one kiss. 'Rilla,' he warned again. But even to his own ears the words sounded more like an invitation than a caution.

'Fine. Looks like I'm just going to have to kiss you instead,' she murmured, her gaze trained on his mouth.

She gave him a beat to deny her. To pull away. To tell her to stop. But he didn't and she could barely see through the haze as she leaned forward, her lips eagerly seeking the heat of his.

Luca pulled back slightly from the kiss, his lips moist from her. Her taste in his mouth, on his tongue. Like a drug. A drug that he wanted more of. Needed more of.

And then they both combusted. Before she knew it Luca was pulling her onto his lap, his fingers clamping onto her thighs, urging them to part so she was straddling him.

And he tasted good and he smelled amazing and she could feel him hard against the barrier of her knickers and she rocked against him to bring his heat closer to hers. She needed him there. The ache was unbearable and she ground her pelvis into his and felt a shudder run right through him.

And they were kissing and kissing and kissing. Kissing like there was no tomorrow. Deep and drugging. Desperate and urgent. And then his hands were on her T-shirt, pulling it over her head, and her nipples brushed against the cotton of his shirt and she moaned out loud at the blatant eroticism. He lowered his mouth and captured an already tortured peak and she cried out at the shaft of pure pleasure that pierced her.

Of their own accord her fingers were at his buttons, surprisingly nimble in their haste to get to his naked chest. And then he was kissing her again and finally, finally his shirt was undone and she could feel the lushness of her breasts squashed against the roughness of his hair. 'Oh, God, Luca,' she moaned against his mouth.

Her words pulled Luca back from the brink a little. They were going too fast. He was being too rough. Like the first time, against the door. She was pregnant now. He needed to be gentle. He needed to go slower.

Damn it all—he should stop. But he'd been

denying himself too long. He just wasn't capable of stopping.

'Rilla,' he whispered, pulling away from her mouth, hushing her whimper, kissing her nose, her forehead, her cheek, stroking her lips, kissing the corner of her mouth.

'Hush… Slow down…slow down,' he murmured, fighting for control of his breath as he stroked her arms, brushed the sides of her breasts, rubbed her back, pulling her into him.

'Oh, Luca, please, don't do this. Don't stop now,' Rilla pleaded, her face on his neck as she desperately scrambled for breath. If he left her like this, she'd go mad. She was too aroused. Had wanted it for too long.

Luca lifted her head away from his shoulder and looked into her eyes, glazed with need. He brushed her hair back from her face. 'I'm not stopping. It's just…it's too fast. I'm too out of control. The baby… I need to be gentle.'

Rilla was fairly out of control herself. Her breath was laboured, her hands trembled, her pelvis ached unbearably, but she knew what a big leap this was for Luca. He had been adamant this wouldn't happen at all. Now he was telling her he couldn't stop it. Didn't want to. But he wanted to try and contain it as much as possible.

Rilla nodded and kissed his lips gently. 'OK,' she whispered, raining kisses over his face. 'OK.'

Her hands went to his fly and she deftly undid the button.

'*Dio!* Rilla.' Luca grabbed her wrist.

'Shh, it's OK.' She gave him a slow, deep kiss full of smothered heat and leashed passion. 'Slow.' She kissed him again. 'I know.' Another kiss. 'It's OK. I know.'

Her hands were stroking him through the fabric of his trousers and he was dizzy with the sensation. Her tawny gaze was begging him to trust her and he leaned back on his hands, her naked breasts glorious with the light playing across them and he shut his eyes and gave himself up to her.

Rilla eased down his zip and freed him from the confines of his underwear. His deep groan empowered her as she revelled in the velvety length of him.

'Rilla.'

Her name came out desperately as he pushed off his hands and gathered her closer, grasping her buttocks in both hands, bringing her centre into intimate contact with his. His mouth closed over a nipple and she held his head, sucking in her breath fast as his teeth grazed the sensitive peak.

There was no easy way to remove the lacy barrier of fabric separating them without her moving, and Rilla knew she wasn't capable of that. She eased the fabric aside and gripped Luca's shoulders hard as his erection nudged at her.

'Easy,' Luca groaned as he felt her heat slowly surround him. He buried his face in her neck as every cell in his body ground to a halt.

'I know,' Rilla gasped as she stretched slowly around his passive penetration. It felt so good. God help her, it felt so good.

He slid up into her with unbearable slowness until she had taken him all and then neither of them moved. All that could be heard was their ragged breathing. Even the Christmas music had faded totally into the background.

Rilla moved slightly and she felt her internal muscles contract. She was so close.

'Easy,' Luca said again, gripping her hips, hard, determined to keep it slow and steady.

'Luca,' Rilla pleaded. She needed to move. Or he did. She was so close. And by the way his skin trembled beneath her touch, she knew he was too.

'Shh,' Luca whispered as he kissed her neck, her collar-bone, his fingers stroking her back. 'It's OK. Let me.' He moved slightly and moaned against her skin as her muscles gripped him hard.

Rilla felt him move again and she moved with him, once, then twice, setting up a torturous rhythm that stoked and sated, stoked and sated.

Luca breathed into her neck, breathing the essence of their joining as they became locked in the sensations they were creating. Cocooned in their embrace, moving as one, feeling as one. Joined in the most intimate way possible.

Their climaxes came quickly despite Luca's

deliberate measured pace. Rilla cried out his name, her fingernails digging into his shoulders, and he joined her seconds later. They shuddered together, the flickering Christmas-tree lights melding into a kaleidoscope of colours behind half-shuttered lids as petty earthly restraints fell away and they soared to new heights.

It was minutes before either of them spoke. Minutes for the last spasms of pleasure to fade and die. Minutes before their pulses settled and their breathing returned to normal.

'Are you OK?' Luca asked, one hand splayed against the small of her back and one on her hip.

She nodded, Luca shifted and she was surprised when he laid her down on her side facing the tree, adjusting the cushion for their heads, and snuggled in behind her.

'Luca?'

'Shh.' Luca kissed her neck. He didn't have the answers to any questions. 'Go to sleep.'

Rilla sighed. Whatever the catalyst had been for tonight, she was just going to be grateful it happened. Her eyes drifted shut, the glorious sight of the tree lighting the darkened room in front of her and the even more glorious feel of Luca behind her.

CHAPTER NINE

RILLA woke at seven, a half-dressed Luca still enfolding her in his embrace. She lay there unmoving. Bing still played in the background and the tree lights still flicked on and off. The gaily wrapped presents at eye level were temptingly tactile and she reached out a hand and ran her fingers over the pile.

A little thrill ran through her and she sighed happily as she snuggled her bottom in closer to him.

'Don't do that,' Luca growled, coming slowly awake as his body leapt ahead of him. He was more than ready to go again and his hand tightened around her waist.

A smile split her face. 'What? This?' she asked innocently, and wriggled again.

Luca sucked in a breath as his morning

erection twitched painfully. He rolled on his back, releasing her. 'Yes, that.'

Rilla looked over her shoulder and grinned at him, rolling over to snuggle into his side, her head on his chest. She lay there for a few moments, resisting the urge to slide her hand down his torso, and it slowly dawned on her she didn't feel sick.

Yes, the morning sickness had improved of late but it had still been there. But there was nothing. She felt...normal. She grinned. This was turning out to be a great Christmas. She raised herself up on her elbow. 'I don't feel sick,' she said to Luca.

Luca frowned. 'Really?'

'Really.' She smiled, tapping his chest with her fingers. 'I feel...great. Do you think this means that it's over? The morning sickness has gone?'

Luca had to admit she looked way better than she had any morning to date. Although no doubt the sated female look that still smouldered in her amber gaze and was stamped all over her face also contributed.

'Well, you're fourteen weeks. It's highly possible. Don't count your chickens, though,' Luca warned, subconsciously reaching out a hand to stroke her shoulder. 'It might not mean anything.'

He smiled to soften the warning. She was looking relaxed and sexy and he didn't want to spoil any faint glimmer of hope she was harbouring. In fact, the desire to roll her on her back and repeat last night's performance was growing more appealing by the second and he dropped his hand from her shoulder.

How the hell had they got here?

Continuing from last night would not be a wise move. He didn't know how he felt this morning other than very confused. They'd shared something more than sex last night— something deeper. And it didn't gel with his plans for them. They were both feeling good and it was Christmas. It would be easy to make more of it than it was, to be seduced back into old habits. Ones that had been disastrous the first time around.

He'd actually felt like they were establishing

the foundations for a lasting relationship these past few weeks. One that could work for their unconventional situation. And he didn't want sex to take over like it had last time, and blur the edges. Even if it was amazing and he wanted her again very badly.

'Anyway,' Luca said, vaulting into a sitting position and displacing her, 'I'm going to hit the shower and go into work for a while. We don't all have a day off.'

Rilla admired the breadth of his naked back, wishing he were totally nude so she could admire all of him. How would he react if she got into the shower with him? The way he was avoiding her gaze told her he was wary and unsure about last night and she'd be wise not to push.

She watched him walk away, a mix of emotions running through her. She loved him. In the dark last night it had been easy to hide from, easy to pass off as sexual attraction, but in the full light of day it was obvious. She loved him. In fact, she'd never stopped.

She'd been lying to herself for seven years

about being over him. Kidded herself that the chance to reconcile had been just for the baby when in reality, deep down, she'd been hoping he would grow to love her again.

But not in the way he had loved her before. Her love for him was so much more complex now. It had grown, evolved into something bigger and better than what they'd had eight years ago. Back then everything had been rosy and bright, and loving him had been easy. Now everything had changed. The stakes were much higher and loving him hurt. Losing him then had been devastating, losing him now would be…unimaginable.

Rilla wished she knew what he was thinking. Last night had been more than just sex for him too, she was sure of it. But he wasn't confessing his undying love for her this morning either. What if it was only ever a chemistry thing for him? What if she had to accept that what they'd had was truly dead for Luca and it was never going to come back?

Could she? Their relationship was so much better than it had been all those years ago.

Fuller, rounder, more complete. Surely she could live happily and be stimulated for years, sharing her life and their baby's life with Luca like this. But would it kill her little by little not to have her love reciprocated? To have him stare at her with lust but never love?

Would that eventually break her or could she go on for the sake of the baby and their family and learn to live with whatever crumbs he threw her way? Learn that being desired was better than nothing at all?

Rilla sighed, her heavy thoughts temporarily sidelined by a need to go to the bathroom. She moved to obey her body's dictates reluctantly. Somehow she felt that if she lay here in this spot for ever, their glorious Christmas tree towering above her, the angel watching over her, the memory of their love-making fresh, then anything was possible between them.

In the cool brightness of the white-tiled bathroom, she knew she'd been right. She should have stayed put. Not moved. Held on to the first glow of rekindled love, that precious moment of peace and goodwill, for as long as she could. She stared at her briefs in disbelief. She was spotting.

Rilla's brain refused to function for a minute. All she could do was stare at the bright spots of blood.

No. Please, no. Not again. Not my baby. I can't live through this again.

Rilla felt as if her throat was closing up as tears clogged her nose and eyes. She felt as if someone had taken a huge carving knife and pierced her through the heart. She clutched at her stomach.

No. Not my baby. Don't take my baby again. This couldn't be happening again. Not the morning after they'd made love. *Not at all!*

She couldn't do this again. She thought about all the tragic women she had nursed throughout the years, coming into the department on their fourth and fifth and sixth miscarriages, and she just didn't know how they went on. This would kill her. And if it didn't, it should. How could she go on living after such a loss?

'You OK in there?'

Rilla startled, swiping at her tear-stained face. 'Y-yes. I'll be out in a moment.'

Luca. Oh, God, how was Luca going to take it? She couldn't live through that look on his face again. Through him withdrawing from her when he'd been so open. It would destroy her this time. Her love for him was tenfold and his rejection would annihilate her completely.

She remembered how he had tried to hold back last night and his gentleness when he hadn't been able to, concerned about the baby. How climbing a ladder or lifting anything heavier than a paperclip raised his ire. How he insisted she put her feet up after work. How he soothed her every morning crooning sweet Italian nothings about their baby and how it was all going to be worthwhile.

Damn it. Damn it. Damn it. Think, think, think. But she couldn't, everything was frozen. Her breath, her pulse, her brain function.

Luca kept up a steady stream of conversation before he left for work and how she managed to act normally, like her whole world wasn't falling apart, she had no idea. She needed time to think and was pleased when he left.

She paced for half an hour around the house,

tears streaming down her face, her brain alternating between assurances that it was nothing and complete shutdown as the worst-case scenario kept rearing its ugly head.

She should call someone, but who? *Think, damn it, think!*

The truth was, the only person she wanted was Luca. No one else knew more intimately than him what she was going through right now, and she wanted nothing other than to be folded in his arms and have him tell her it was going to be OK.

But what if he had that look in his eyes like last time? She had gone to him first too, seven years ago, in the mistaken belief he would be there for her. That they would be there for each other. And that had been a disaster.

No! They'd come so far since those early days. Their relationship was much stronger, built on more than sex and a whirlwind fairy-tale. It had a more solid foundation. They were so much better equipped today to deal with something like this. Weren't they?

But what if they weren't? What if Luca was truly only interested in her because she was carrying his child? What if he never was going to grow to love her again? What if she lost the baby and he walked away again too? Just because their love-making last night had seemed exactly that—*love*-making—it didn't mean he was in love with her or that he felt anything at all for her other than insane desire and propriety because she was the mother of his child.

She sat on the lounge and buried her face in her hands, hot tears trekking down her face as she rocked back and forth. She was so scared. Terrified of losing another baby and frightened of losing Luca, like last time. Her heart told her to go to him, seek him out, but she was confused. If she was losing this baby, she couldn't put her heart on the line as well.

Hailey. She could ring Hailey. She was a midwife. Rilla rose, lifted the phone off the hook and dialled her sister's number with shaky hands.

'Hello, Hailey speaking.'

'Hailey.' Rilla tried to keep the wobble out of her voice—unsuccessfully. Hailey's chirpy greeting had put her on shaky ground.

'Ril? What's wrong?'

Rilla took some deep breaths. 'I'm bleeding.' There was a pause during which Rilla gripped the phone hard and concentrated on her breathing. 'Hails?'

'OK. Right. Don't panic. What do you mean, bleeding? Full-on flow with clots or just spotting?'

Rilla sniffled and wiped her nose on a tissue. 'Spotting.'

'OK, well, that's good. Spotting isn't unusual at this stage. It can be hormonal or from the cervix softening. Have you got any cramping?'

Rilla remembered the cramping from last time. The feeling that her insides were being put through a blender. 'No,' she sniffled, feeling the first ray of optimism shine through the bleakness inside her.

'That's good. That's really good, Ril.'

Rilla felt fresh tears well at her sister's overly bright response. Hails had witnessed the devastation of the first miscarriage and Rilla knew she was trying really hard to allay her fears and she clung to Hailey's positivity.

'How about your morning sickness? How's that going?'

Rilla felt the slender thread Hailey had handed her snap and the bleakness envelop her. 'It's gone! This morning I woke up and I haven't thrown up at all. Haven't even felt like it! I was so relieved.'

Rilla wiped away a fresh batch of tears, castigating her foolishness. She should have known it was something sinister—not a cause to celebrate. 'This is bad, isn't it? My hormone levels have plummeted because I'm...' She choked on the words. 'The baby's dead.'

'No, Ril. No. Not necessarily. What does Luca think?'

Rilla felt another hot wave of tears course down her cheeks. How could she explain to her younger sister the complexities of their screwed-up relationship? Everyone thought they were happily reconciled. 'I haven't told him. I can't.'

A harebrained scheme formed in her brain. 'Can you meet me at the General?'

'Of course.'

'You can draw some blood and we can get the old portable ultrasound out.'

'I don't know, Ril. I think you need to talk to Luca about this.'

Rilla felt a block of emotion rise in her throat, constricting her breathing. 'I have to know if there's a heartbeat or not, Hailey. You don't understand… Last time…last time was awful. I don't know if we can survive another… Please, I just have to know.'

'Ril…'

She heard the doubt in her sister's voice but she couldn't talk to Luca about this. Not before she knew herself. 'Please, Hails. Please.'

'OK, give me half an hour.'

Rilla swallowed the lump in her throat and thanked the universe for sisters. 'Perfect.'

She threw some clothes on, pulled her hair back in a quick ponytail, snatched her keys up and was out of the house in under five minutes.

Carols played on the radio on the way to the General and Rilla didn't even notice. She was frozen inside. She clutched her stomach as she drove and begged the universe for everything to be OK. There was still no cramping and the bleeding was only scanty, but she was bargaining for all she was worth. And the only bargaining chip she had was her love for Luca.

Please let the baby be OK and I'll live with him in name only and never ask for anything more. Please, let the baby be OK and I'll never lust after him again. Please, let the baby be OK and I won't ask for Luca to love me.

The words ran like a mantra through her head and nothing else existed.

She screeched into the hospital car park a few minutes later and Rilla despaired at how far away she had to park. Every step jolted her and she fretted about the impact on a baby that might already be preparing to leave the womb.

Rilla lurked around the entrance and was pleased to see Hailey walking towards her ten minutes later.

'Ril?' Hailey said, embracing her sister. 'How are you now?'

Rilla hugged back, squeezing Hailey tight.

'Terrible.' She swallowed. 'I'm sorry to drag you out like this so early on your day off.'

'Oh, babe,' Hailey said. 'I bet it's nothing. Let's think positively, OK?'

Rilla nodded, the lump in her throat too big to speak, clinging to Hailey's optimism like a life jacket in stormy seas.

They entered the department, Rilla checking the coast was clear before shutting them in the empty triage room behind the desk, where patients were assessed privately.

She handed Hailey a tourniquet. 'Draw some blood. Let's get a beta HCG level off first.'

Hailey had just plunged the needle into the crook of Rilla's arm when the door opened abruptly and the sisters startled at the unexpected intrusion. Luca stood in the doorway, his mouth open in mid-sentence. Rilla froze. She wanted simultaneously to screech at him to go away and run crying into his arms.

Luca's thoughts churned madly as he shut the door. Rilla's eyes were red and puffy, her olive complexion blotchy. Something was wrong. The beginnings of dread and anger burnt in his gut. Why was she here with her sister? Why hadn't she come to him? 'What the hell's going on here?'

Hailey looked from one to the other. She withdrew the needle from Rilla's vein and plunged it into the vacu-tainer, watching as the blood was sucked out of the syringe. 'I'm going to leave you two to chat,' she said, gathering the blood tube and a lab specimen bag. 'Unless you want me to stay?'

'No. Thanks, Hails.' She squeezed her sister's hand reassuringly. 'It'll be fine.' Even though Luca looked really angry and she didn't think it was going to be fine at all. 'Can you mark it urgent?'

Luca was silent as Hailey left. 'What's happened?' He braced himself to be told she was having another miscarriage. That they were losing this baby too.

'I started spotting this morning.'

Luca's breath left his chest in an explosive hiss. A crippling sense of déjà vu swamped him as he fumbled for a chair and sat, his head in his

hands. 'I knew it. I knew I shouldn't have suc-
cumbed last night.'

Rilla put her hand out to comfort him. He
sounded so disgusted with himself. It wasn't his
fault and she couldn't bear to hear him blame
himself. It was like last time all over again.
'Luca, don't…'

He stood, shrugging her hand off his shoulder,
cursing himself. He didn't deserve her under-
standing. He thumped his closed fist against the
bench. 'Damn it.'

Rilla braced herself. He paced and she
watched him and waited for the post-mortem to
commence. She felt so lonely and utterly miserable and remembered as if it were yesterday
how isolated she'd felt as Luca had withdrawn
from her a little more each day.

But this was worse because she'd allowed that
part of herself that had been paralysed by him
leaving seven years ago to come to life again.
Waiting for him to sever the cord was agony and
she felt cold all over.

Luca could feel a familiar sense of powerless-
ness creep over him and he pushed it away ruth-

lessly. They were not going to repeat the mistakes of seven years ago. His medical brain took over. Spotting did not have to mean anything.

He turned to face Rilla. She looked wretched and his heart swelled for her. 'Don't,' he said, walking towards her. He lifted a hand and stroked a finger down the side of her face, lingering at the freckle adorning the corner of her mouth. 'It'll be OK,' he crooned, and pulled her into an embrace.

Rilla hadn't known what he'd do or say but this certainly hadn't been on her list of possibilities. He wasn't pushing her away. It felt so heavenly to be safe in the circle of his arms and so unexpected that she burst into tears. She wanted to tell him she loved him but she was crying too hard to say anything.

'We're not going to jump to conclusions,' he murmured, stroking her back as she cried. 'It's probably nothing.'

Rilla clung to him. She wanted to believe him. She really did. Where had this Luca been seven years ago?

'We're going to go to my office and get out

the old portable ultrasound machine and have a look. OK?'

Rilla nodded. His voice was low and comforting, his body swaying gently back and forth with hers. Her love for him was a tight painful knot in her chest. *Please, let Luca be right. Please, let our baby be OK.*

Luca led her to his office and urged her to sit on the lounge. 'I'll be back. I'll grab the machine and see if the lab results are back yet, OK?'

Rilla nodded, trying not to think that within minutes she'd know the fate of their baby. She remembered the bargain she'd made in the car and repeated her promise to give up Luca's love in exchange for the baby's life. It would be hard but the alternative didn't bear thinking about.

A few minutes later Luca wheeled in a metal trolley housing a machine not much bigger than a video recorder with a screen only about ten centimetres square. It was too old and basic for any in-depth sonography but was a very quick, handy diagnostic tool for foetal heartbeats.

'What did the lab say?' Rilla asked, blowing her nose.

'They're in the process of doing it. I gave the lab tech my extension number to ring the results through.'

Luca placed the trolley beside the couch and squatted beside her. He gave her hand a squeeze. 'Lie back,' he said huskily.

Rilla did as he asked, pulling up her grey T-shirt, unzipping and slipping down her cargo pants until they gave Luca an unrestricted view. She stared at the ceiling, trying really, really hard not to cry. She couldn't look at the screen, she just couldn't. The cool gel landed on her skin and she flinched.

'Sorry,' Luca murmured.

Rilla shut her eyes hard, wiping away a tear that squeezed out from behind her lids. It didn't matter. What was a bit of cold gel? If she was losing this baby, nothing would matter ever again. She felt the probe down low on her stomach and clenched her fists, waiting to hear the verdict.

Luca took a couple of deep breaths. He

glanced at Rilla lying there rigidly and knew exactly how she felt. Could he bear to look at the screen and see his precious baby had died? Was he capable of delivering the bad news to her if he couldn't find the heartbeat?

His hand shook as the probe rolled across the skin of Rilla's abdomen. He could barely hear anything over the roar of his pulse in his ears. It took him seconds to locate what he was after. Seconds more for the visual information to penetrate his suddenly paralysed brain.

A strong central flicker beating away merrily.

Luca shut his eyes as relief slowly washed through his system and when he opened them again he was on steadier emotional ground. Their baby was safe.

'There it is,' he murmured, his eyes glued to the screen, the movement compelling. 'One strong little heartbeat.'

Rilla's eyes flew open, her head lifted, seeking the small screen eagerly. He was right—there it was. It was blurry and fuzzy but it was most definitely a very wriggly baby-shaped form, all head and bones, with a steady central flicker. Rilla felt her breath hiss noisily from her lungs. She didn't dare hope.

She looked at Luca. 'What if it's clinging on for dear life, beating madly, fighting against the inevitable pull?'

The phone rang and Luca reached over to pick it up with his spare hand, using his shoulder to hold it in place while he kept the probe positioned with the other.

Rilla didn't even hear the conversation as her body systems gradually came back on line. She stared and stared at the image, finding the flickering mesmerising. It didn't falter.

Luca replaced the phone, a huge grin on his face. 'That was the lab. Your beta HCG is through the roof. No wonder you've been so ill. This is a very viable baby.'

'But I've stopped feeling sick. Just like that. Just like a switch flipping,' Rilla persisted.

Luca shrugged. 'Well, put it down to an early Christmas gift from the baby. I wouldn't count on it lasting too long.'

Rilla's head fell back against the couch, relief swamping her with a deluge of emotions. She smiled and then she laughed and then before she knew it her face had completely crumpled and a sob had escaped her mouth.

'Hey,' Luca chided. His gaze met Rilla's and he felt an overwhelming wave of emotion sweep up over him.

It was too intense to analyse but he knew it was about more than her being the mother of his child. And it was almost impossible to resist. He wanted to gather her into his arms and hold her tight. He dropped the transducer and hauled her against him.

'Oh, Luca,' Rilla choked, wiping at the hot tears that fell unabated from her eyes. 'I thought I was losing… We were… I was so scared.'

'I know,' he said. 'I know.' He'd been pretty damn scared himself.

'I thought I was being p-punished again.'

Luca frowned. 'Punished? Don't be silly. For what?'

Rilla shook her head. It didn't matter. She'd never said anything to Luca about it last time. Never told anyone. Hadn't ever planned to. It had just slipped out in the emotional landslide triggered by the deluge of relief that had swept thought her system.

'It's nothing,' she dismissed, her voice still thick with tears.

'Rilla.' He set her back from him a bit and swept the loose hair that had fallen from her hasty ponytail back from her face. 'It wasn't your fault. Nothing either of us did caused the miscarriage.'

Rilla shook her head. 'No, you don't understand.' There was one thing she had never told him, had tried to forget herself. But she'd borne it for so long now she just needed to get it out. She mentally prepared herself for Luca's recoil but she couldn't bear the burden of it any longer. 'Back then…when…' She took a deep breath. 'A part of me didn't want the baby.'

Rilla shut her eyes to block out the look of horror she knew she'd see on Luca's face. He'd wanted the baby right from the start.

'Oh, Rilla,' Luca said, softly and wiped at a tear as it trekked down her cheek.

She opened her eyes. 'I was so young and we were just married.' Rilla choked on a sob. 'I *was* happy about it… It was just a shock…and I'd hoped we'd have more time together as a couple and I didn't know if I'd be any good at it. And then…'

Luca's heart went out to her. 'Oh, Rilla. Rilla, Rilla,' he crooned. She'd been blaming herself all these years over a perfectly normal reaction to an unplanned pregnancy. 'I felt the same way,' he confessed.

Rilla blinked. 'You…you did?' she sniffled.

He gave her a sad smile. 'I did. I wanted the baby and I was happy but it was very unexpected and it took me a little while to adjust.'

'But…but you were ecstatic about it.' She frowned.

'Because I thought that's what you wanted me to be. But deep down I was a bit panicky. Initially anyway. I got used to the idea very quickly.'

Rilla felt another hot tear roll down her face. 'Same here.'

Luca wiped it away, her sad face too much to bear on such a happy day. 'Hush,' he said as her face crumpled again and he pulled her back into his arms. They'd both carried terrible guilt for too many years. It was good for them both to finally have it out there.

He held her for a long time, until her sobbing abated and she lay quietly within his embrace. He gently eased away from her. 'Feel better now?' he asked.

Rilla nodded. She felt immeasurably lighter. To know that Luca had gone through similar feelings had been an epiphany. Why, oh, why hadn't they turned to each other back then, instead of being too ashamed and guilty to admit their true feelings?

Luca's shirt had a sticky wet patch where he'd collected some of the gel off Rilla's stomach. He pulled a tissue out of the box that was sitting on the bottom of the trolley and pushed Rilla gently back against the couch so he could wipe the remaining goo off her.

As his hands stroked over her stomach he was excruciatingly aware his child was beneath it and they'd just had a very close call. He placed his hand on her stomach. 'Do you mind?' he asked huskily.

Rilla's breath caught in her throat as she

shook her head and watched Luca lower his head to her stomach and drop gentle, reverent kisses across her abdomen.

'There is nothing in this world more important to me than you,' he murmured to the life beneath, Rilla's skin soft against his mouth. 'I will devote all my life to loving you and looking after you.'

Rilla pushed her fingers into his hair, his dark head near her belly, talking quietly to their baby, so very intimate. Her heart overflowed with love for him.

'And your mother. I will look after her as well.'

Luca glanced up at Rilla and her skin tingled where his whiskers had grazed. His eyes shone with love, but not the kind she wanted, and her heart almost broke in two.

There is nothing in this world more important to me than you.

His exact words. He loved the baby, that much was plain. But her? Only as the mother of his child.

'How can I ever thank you for giving me such a precious gift?' Luca murmured.

Love me. Love me, damn you.

Rilla felt a lump rise in her throat. But she knew with a sickening reality their relationship would only ever be about the baby for Luca. That she'd never see him look at her with such loving tenderness. That he may desire her but he was saving all his love for their baby. And he'd never given her any reason to believe otherwise.

She'd been living in some fantasy land where Luca was going to eventually realise he still loved her and sweep her off her feet again. But as his big hand warmed her stomach it was blatantly obvious she was never going to be anything other than the mother of his child. A life-support system for a womb.

Rilla sat up, displacing his hands. She fumbled with the zip, her heart pounding, her course becoming clearer and clearer. She had bartered her love for Luca with the universe for her baby's life but she realised now it had been an impossible bargain. She could never not love him. And she certainly couldn't be with him if he didn't love her.

Her life stretched before her interminably. A loveless marriage. Putting on an act for their child and a brave face for the rest of the world. 'I can't do this, Luca. I'm sorry, I thought I could but I can't.'

Luca frowned and rocked back onto his heels. 'What do you mean? Can't do what?'

'This,' she said, standing and moving away from him. 'Us. Let's face it, if it wasn't for this baby there'd be no reconciliation. I'm just a walking womb to you. And that's fine, you never promised me anything else. But I can't do it.'

Luca felt as if she had slapped him. *Dio!* He felt the first pulse of anger enter his circulation. 'No! You're wrong.' How could she think that? After these last weeks? If that was what she really thought, there was no hope for them.

Rilla gave a harsh laugh and swallowed another ball of tears that threatened. The more she thought about it, the more convinced she became. And the more convinced, the more depressed.

Surely she deserved a full, mature relationship? How had she thought she could ever settle for less?

'How can you deny it, Luca? Everything you do, every decision you make, centres around the baby. Even when we made love last night, when I was out of my mind with wanting you, all you could think about was how to do it so it was safest for the baby. Face it—I'm just a receptacle for your child,' she said miserably. 'A warm body for it to grow in.'

'Rilla, no!' Luca denied quickly. How could she think such a thing? He felt…he felt… Damn it. He didn't know how he felt, but she made him sound so callous. 'I'm sorry I have made you feel like that and if you're worried about how I will be with you after the baby is born, please don't be,' he hastened to assure her.

'We will always need you. I will always treat you with the utmost courtesy and respect, as befitting the mother of my child.'

Rilla couldn't decide if she wanted to cry or scream. She didn't want his saintly devotion to her mothering skills, his platonic companionship. The mere thought was as depressing as hell. She wanted him to love her and all the highs and lows that brought with it.

'And what if I don't want that, Luca? What if I want you to disrespect me sometimes? What if I don't want you to be polite and courteous? What if I want more?'

Luca frowned. What the hell was with her? Were the hormones making her insane? Was this about sex again? Her breasts were heaving an agitated rhythm within the confines of her T-shirt and suddenly he was thinking about sex even if she wasn't. *He really needed to get that under control.*

'But, Rilla…' he said carefully, not sure of the woman who sat before him with red eyes and a beseeching gaze. She looked fifty per cent crazed and one hundred per cent desirable, and he didn't know much about where this conversation was heading or what it was really about, but he knew he had to tread delicately. 'We agreed that this was going to be about the baby.'

Rilla felt a sharp pain in her chest and rubbed at it absently. It hurt. It hurt inside so much. She knew she must look a sight. She was crying again, wiping at her eyes uselessly as more tears spilled out. 'I know, I know that's what we agreed.'

Luca reached for her and she put out her hands to ward him off. 'No, Luca.' If he touched her now, she'd agree to anything. She had to stay strong.

Luca felt completely useless. Rilla was an emotional wreck, no doubt a delayed reaction to the fright she'd just had and all he wanted to do was hold her, but she was so mad at him for some reason.

What on earth was she going on about? He only cared about her because she was the mother of his child? That he only thought of her as a receptacle? Didn't she know that, try as he may to keep to their bargain, she got under his skin? He didn't know what she wanted or how to comfort her.

'Damn it, Rilla, what do you want?'

I need you to love me, you fool.

Oh, God, was he that dense, that closed off to her he couldn't see? She took some deep breaths. 'I want you to sign the divorce papers. We can work out some parenting agreement that suits us both, but I can't live with you, Luca.'

Luca reeled from her demand as if hit by a

physical force. *No!* He didn't want a damn divorce. If he'd wanted one he would have initiated proceedings a long time ago or signed the papers when they'd arrived.

He stared at her, willing her to take the words back. They'd been getting on so well. Getting to know each other over again. Building a life together. He thought she'd been happy. He'd begun to hope that maybe one day they could be even more. Was a future with him that bad?

He wanted to shake her but she was standing there crying, looking utterly wretched, and he felt impotent. Like after the miscarriage, when he'd known she'd been hurting but hadn't known how to reach her. He couldn't bear to put her through that again.

'Fine, damn it,' he snapped, and strode to his desk. The divorce papers had been sitting there since his return. He yanked open the drawer and pulled them out. 'Is this what you want?'

He looked at her and waited for her to deny it. To tell him she was tired and hormonal and not to be silly. But she nodded her head, despite looking even more miserable. He picked up a pen from his desk and signed in the indicated places.

Rilla watched in abject misery. This was it. It was over. Luca was as mad as hell if his bold, angry slashes were any gauge, but it was better than companionship and a platonic marriage.

Luca seethed as he signed. More than seethed, he realised his whole world was breaking apart. Every fibre of his being was urging him not to sign. Damn it, of course she meant more to him than a vessel for the baby she was giving him. He wanted her also, he couldn't help it. But that was desire. That was sex.

But even as he protested he knew it was wrong. It was so much more than desire. She had always held his heart. It was why he still wore his wedding ring seven years down the track. Why he hadn't been with another woman despite numerous offers. Why he hadn't filed for divorce. Why he hadn't signed the papers. Why just receiving the papers had sent him posthaste to the other side of the world.

Dio! He still loved her. How could he have been so blind? He'd been treating her as a mother figure in order to keep his distance from her and protect his heart, but it hadn't worked. He looked ahead to a future without her, a future these blasted papers would ensure, and the urge to tear them up possessed him.

He straightened, gathered them together lest he act on his impulse, and held them out to Rilla. She was crying quietly, looking like she had just lost a million dollars, not been given the one thing she'd said she wanted.

What if I want you to disrespect me some-times? What if I want more?

Her words came back to him. That's what she'd said and she was looking at the papers as if he'd signed them in a pen dipped in poison. Had she acted so demented and cried so much because she didn't want the damn papers at all? Because she still loved him too?

Did he dare hope? 'Are you sure, Rilla?' he asked, his voice husky, holding on to one end of the papers as she held on to the other. 'Are you absolutely sure?'

Rilla didn't know how much more she could stand. She'd cried a bucketload that morning but there was so much more to come and she knew she wasn't far away from completely breaking down.

Luca could feel her grip loosening on the papers and see she was wavering. 'We've done so many things wrong, Rilla. Let's at least do something right. Let's be honest with each other. Once and for all.'

Rilla felt her heart flop in her chest. What did he mean? He was looking at her, his dark gaze earnest, and there was something unreadable in it. Whatever it was, it was intense. Dared she hope? She let go of the papers and sank into one of his office chairs.

Luca faced her, his love for her swelling inside him.

'I've been such a fool. I told myself I was over you and that we could make this about the baby but I was wrong. Yes, I want this baby, and I'll no doubt still be unbearably over-protective and nag you when you lift anything heavy and fuss around making sure you're eating properly. But I'm the father, it's my job. My father wasn't there for me so I'm going to be there for my child. Like a lion watching over his pride. I'm sorry if you don't like that about me, but it's who I am.'

Rilla felt goose-bumps break out on her arms and she rubbed them absently. Of course she wanted Luca to be a strong father. Watchful and protective, but not to the exclusion of all else. Not pushing her out of the pride in the process.

'I love you, Rilla. I never stopped. I want us to live together as husband and wife, in the truest sense of the word. No more sham. I had seven years without you and I was utterly miserable. I don't want to waste any more time pretending I'm not in love with you when, in fact, the love I felt for you has grown and matured and is so much bigger than it ever was before.'

She stared at him, his speech slowly sinking in. His words of love and a true marriage were making her dizzy, going straight to her head. So much more than she'd ever hoped for, but she had to be sure of his motivation. 'Because of the baby.'

'No. Not because of the baby. Because of you. I came back to Australia for you.'

Rilla's heart leapt at his words but she still

needed to be sure. She frowned. 'I thought you came back for closure. For the job?'

'I lied to you. Hell, I lied to myself. I came back for you. The divorce papers gave me such a jolt. I started looking for a job in Brisbane the same day. I couldn't believe my luck when I saw the job at the General advertised. I told myself I was coming back for my career and to prove I was over you, but I was lying to myself. I knew it that day in the bush when I noticed you were ring-less and I certainly knew it the day against the door. I just couldn't face it. Couldn't bear to leave my heart so exposed again.'

Rilla gazed into his eyes. They were warm and open. She could see he was telling her the truth. He had come back for her. Before she was pregnant. Even if he hadn't been aware of it. She could see his love and the pain all twisted together in his eyes, and she could hardly breathe as a burst of pure happiness rose inside her.

Luca moved towards her. His grief over the miscarriage and then his stubbornness over this baby had nearly lost her, nearly made him lose track of what was important. He came around to her side of the desk and sank to his knees in front of her.

'I know I don't deserve it but can you ever forgive me, Rilla? Do you think you could love me too?'

Rilla felt a lump rise in her throat. 'Oh, Luca,' she cried, pushing her fingers into his hair and swooping her lips down for a brief hard kiss of his momentarily stunned mouth. 'I love you so much, it hurts. Of course I forgive you. We both made mistakes. We were both stubborn. I thought I was over you too. Why, oh, why, did we waste seven years?'

Luca was just grateful they'd finally got their act together. 'We were fools,' he whispered, and this time he claimed a kiss, wrapping his arms around her waist and pulling her until they were standing pressed together.

'Does this mean you'll be my wife again?' he asked. 'Properly this time?'

Rilla nodded through suddenly glazed vision. 'For ever and ever.'

Luca grinned. 'This is an amazing Christmas.'

'Amen to that.' Rilla grinned back.

EPILOGUE

CHRISTMAS Day at the Winterses' house was full on. Everyone was there, including David and his girlfriend and the newest member of the Winters clan, Bridie. It was a day full of love and laughter.

Despite the soaring summer temperatures, Penny Winters was a traditionalist at heart, which meant lunch was turkey with all the trimmings. The air-conditioning units kept the outside heat at bay and everyone ate to excess.

The usual groans were heard around the table after the last of the pudding was eaten, overindulgence stretching bellies. Rilla, whose morning sickness was all but over, ate everything in sight, making up for lost time, and withstood the good-natured teasing of her siblings.

After lunch they sat around in the lounge,

watching cricket on TV and dozing for a while as carols played in the background. Rilla smiled indulgently at Luca, who was learning the rules of cricket from John. The last two weeks had been the best of her life. She thanked the universe every day that they'd both finally come to their senses.

She heard Bridie stir and as Beth and Gabe were both dozing she picked her up out of her cot. 'Hello, beautiful girl,' she whispered, and was rewarded with a dribbly smile.

Rilla took Bridie out onto the deck. It was quiet outside and she wanted to give Beth and Gabe a proper break. It was hot but the deck was covered and a slight breeze blew through the tall gums and lifted the hair off Rilla's neck.

Luca found her out there ten minutes later. He was blasted with a furnace of heat as he opened the door and he had a fleeting longing for snow-flakes and frozen lakes. But he knew it wasn't a serious desire. This was where he belonged. With Rilla.

She was rocking Bridie and he found the movement mesmerising. She had tinsel in her hair and a zany Christmas T-shirt on and a Santa hat, and she'd never looked more beautiful.

This was how she would look holding their child. Her confident stance, her instinctive rocking, her low, gentle voice. She would make an excellent mother. But first and foremost she was Rilla. His wife. His lover. His soul-mate.

'You're good at that,' he murmured softly. He knew she'd heard him as her rhythm paused briefly before her hips resumed their gentle sway.

'Damn right I am.' She grinned at him. 'Had enough of cricket?'

Luca chuckled as he walked towards her. 'I think it may take me a few years to grasp it. Your father's going to take me to a game some time at the Gabba.'

He put his arm around Rilla, drawing her into his side and looked down at his niece. 'How is my little bush baby?' he murmured.

'Alert,' Rilla said as they both watched Bridie follow the lazy path of Jumbles, the family cat.

They gazed down at her for a long while, a very special connection between the three of them.

Rilla finally dragged her gaze away. 'Hey, guess what?' she asked, indicating above them with a nod of her head.

Luca looked up to see a bunch of bush mistletoe hanging from the middle of the exposed beams of the deck.

'Do you think I need mistletoe to kiss my wife?' He grinned.

'You haven't done it yet,' Rilla teased.

'Well, now, I'll have to do something about that, won't I?' he said, lowering his mouth. 'Merry Christmas, Rilla,' he murmured, his lips touching hers as he formed the words. 'Here's to many, many more.'

'Merry Christmas, Luca.' Rilla sighed, and surrendered to his mouth, knowing they'd finally made it.

MEDICAL™

—⋀— *Large Print* —⋀—

Titles for the next six months…

June

A MUMMY FOR CHRISTMAS	Caroline Anderson
A BRIDE AND CHILD WORTH WAITING FOR	Marion Lennox
ONE MAGICAL CHRISTMAS	Carol Marinelli
THE GP'S MEANT-TO-BE BRIDE	Jennifer Taylor
THE ITALIAN SURGEON'S CHRISTMAS MIRACLE	Alison Roberts
CHILDREN'S DOCTOR, CHRISTMAS BRIDE	Lucy Clark

July

THE GREEK DOCTOR'S NEW-YEAR BABY	Kate Hardy
THE HEART SURGEON'S SECRET CHILD	Meredith Webber
THE MIDWIFE'S LITTLE MIRACLE	Fiona McArthur
THE SINGLE DAD'S NEW-YEAR BRIDE	Amy Andrews
THE WIFE HE'S BEEN WAITING FOR	Dianne Drake
POSH DOC CLAIMS HIS BRIDE	Anne Fraser

August

CHILDREN'S DOCTOR, SOCIETY BRIDE	Joanna Neil
THE HEART SURGEON'S BABY SURPRISE	Meredith Webber
A WIFE FOR THE BABY DOCTOR	Josie Metcalfe
THE ROYAL DOCTOR'S BRIDE	Jessica Matthews
OUTBACK DOCTOR, ENGLISH BRIDE	Leah Martyn
SURGEON BOSS, SURPRISE DAD	Janice Lynn

MILLS & BOON®
Pure reading pleasure™

0509 LP 2P P1 Medical

MEDICAL™

—∿— *Large Print* —∿—

September

THE CHILDREN'S DOCTOR'S SPECIAL PROPOSAL	Kate Hardy
ENGLISH DOCTOR, ITALIAN BRIDE	Carol Marinelli
THE DOCTOR'S BABY BOMBSHELL	Jennifer Taylor
EMERGENCY: SINGLE DAD, MOTHER NEEDED	Laura Iding
THE DOCTOR CLAIMS HIS BRIDE	Fiona Lowe
ASSIGNMENT: BABY	Lynne Marshall

October

A FAMILY FOR HIS TINY TWINS	Josie Metcalfe
ONE NIGHT WITH HER BOSS	Alison Roberts
TOP-NOTCH DOC, OUTBACK BRIDE	Melanie Milburne
A BABY FOR THE VILLAGE DOCTOR	Abigail Gordon
THE MIDWIFE AND THE SINGLE DAD	Gill Sanderson
THE PLAYBOY FIREFIGHTER'S PROPOSAL	Emily Forbes

November

THE SURGEON SHE'S BEEN WAITING FOR	Joanna Neil
THE BABY DOCTOR'S BRIDE	Jessica Matthews
THE MIDWIFE'S NEW-FOUND FAMILY	Fiona McArthur
THE EMERGENCY DOCTOR CLAIMS HIS WIFE	Margaret McDonagh
THE SURGEON'S SPECIAL DELIVERY	Fiona Lowe
A MOTHER FOR HIS TWINS	Lucy Clark

⊚™ MILLS & BOON®
Pure reading pleasure™

0509 LP 2P P2 Medical